The Crossroads Hotel

Volume 2

By Karen Avizur

The Crossroads Hotel: Volume 2

The Crossroads Hotel: Volume 2

Karen Avizur

The Crossroads Hotel: Volume 2

Table of Contents

Karen Avizur

Prologue

Over two years ago, I started a job as the manager of the Crossroads Hotel and Diner. Only recently did I find out I'd died in a car crash the day I'd arrived.

After I'd been told, I felt dazed, like I was wearing a pair of strange-tinted glasses. My boss, a wizard named Mr. Lucero, had suggested I take some time off to adjust. I only took two days, though, before wanting to get back to my routine. I live above the hotel's diner, and only exist as a real person in the few square miles of the crossroads' territory. That meant there wasn't much to distract me from what I was dealing with.

Instead, my coworkers, who are also my closest friends, were there for me every day I came back to that front desk. And it's a good thing I like my job, because stewing in the fact that I'd be at that desk for the rest of my 'life' left me polishing off a bottle of wine by myself more than once. Mr. Lucero also said I could leave early, as soon as Delilah arrived to relieve Josh at 5 p.m., if I wanted to have some more hours in the day to paint. He knows me well. I've only done it a few times, but there were some days that my hands were itching to get a hold of a brush, put paint to canvas, and just let the hours slide by.

My job often has downtime, and while I'm usually sketching something to pass the time, I now found my pencil coming to a stop as my mind wandered. Questions spun in my head, about what my future was going to look like, and since Mr. Lucero had assured me that his door was always open, I went to him for the answers. I wasn't thinking that much about my surroundings; they were non-negotiable. I was thinking about myself.

Was I allowed to have access to Ferromancy Fiber, the internet for nonhumans on Earth that I'd apparently been selling my artwork on for two years? The answer was a hard no. I was human. A dead one, but still human. I'd continue to interface through websites I already used, including Etsy.

Could I become noncorporeal, or even invisible? Come on, of course I asked him that. Mr. Lucero said it was likely, but he didn't recommend messing around with those kinds of experiments right away, considering how unnecessary they were.

What would happen if I got injured? That was the one that finally gave me good news. Turns out I simply have to focus on the fact that my body is a construct and paper cuts fade away. The pain and damage of a stubbed toe as well, which is handy. I haven't had to test it on anything severe, but I'm a literal manifestation of who I was, so there's no reason there should be anything I couldn't recover from.

There is no spoon.

And my appearance? Whether or not I'd stop aging sometime soon was my decision, apparently, but for now, everything in me was telling me to live as if I were still alive. That included growing.

I wish I could talk to the crossroads. There are a few big questions I have for it. But that's not how these things work, because it may be sentient enough to keep people and things from coming in or going out, but it's not the type to hold a conversation. How would you even communicate with a road? I had this surreal image of me holding a séance in the middle of the intersection. Drawing a pentagram and summoning its corporeal form with a scrap of tire, a piece of a taillight, some motor oil, a mason jar of truck exhaust, and a single shoe.

So, I just hugged my friends, I slept, I ate Andrea's fantastic cooking, and most importantly, I kept going into my art room to turn blank canvases into wonderful paintings.

Also, I kept working at this job twelve hours a day, six days a week. Because this is a special hotel that often has special guests. And what better way to help me feel like nothing had changed than to have an upcoming week where we'd be fully booked for a convention of nonhumans?

Karen Avizur

Chapter 1

"Acustomer ordered *tarantulas.*"
I was standing behind the front desk and had been ready to hear anything from the woman who had stormed up with a complaint. Now, I paused for a beat. "Can you clarify that for me?" I asked. In this hotel, that was always a great question to both buy me time to think and to get more information. Especially when it came to an issue between a local and a not-so-local guest in our diner.

Her gaze narrowed. "He ordered fried tarantulas, and the waitress came out with a plateful of them, and now he's crunching away! The waitress knew him by name!"

Well, can't get more straightforward than that. "All right. Well, our chef is known for being extremely talented at her job, which brings a wide variety of customers to the diner. And many of them come back and become regulars."

The woman's face contorted. "But he's…eating…spiders," she told me, as if that explained everything.

I nodded. "Fried tarantulas are a delicacy in Cambodia."

That silenced her, and she looked like she was buffering. I could imagine her thinking, *'But we're not in Cambodia'*. The thing was, this intersection got visitors from all over, and I don't mean just from our plane of existence. Whoever this guest was might be from Cambodia or might have nothing to do with the country. It's just that I couldn't help but google 'fried tarantulas' the first time this had happened, so I learned that fun fact.

I felt my coworker's presence next to me, being decidedly quiet. Josh could handle guest issues by this point in his work tenure, but these issues were best handled one-on-one. And this saved the inevitable hassle of me entering the conversation when they saw my name tag said Manager. At least this woman wasn't like the last complainer, stuck on the idea that our kitchen needed to be swept top to bottom by the health department.

"I cannot listen to that crunching," she finally hissed at me.

"That's fine, completely understandable," I replied, nodding. Motioning to my right, I gestured toward the couches and loveseats, and the tables in front of them. "Feel free to bring your meal out to eat in the lobby. Or you could sit out at the picnic table in front of the building. I know it's warm out, but it's situated in the shade of the building at this time of day."

Her shoulders lowered an inch or so and she hesitated before nodding. "Can you...can you ask them to bring my food out to the lobby?"

"Of course," I said with a smile. "I can bring it out for you myself."

With a sigh, she walked over to one of the couches and put her purse down, leaning back and staring into space. Glancing to Josh briefly, and seeing the shadow of a smile on his face, I walked around the end of the reception desk, through the gap between it and the wall. In the diner, I spotted the only booth with food that was unoccupied, a meal of roast chicken and veggies, and I placed the utensils on the plate. Then I tucked a few napkins under the plate between my fingers and took the drink in my other hand.

I only needed to meet our server Jodie's gaze meaningfully for a moment. She smiled subtly and nodded.

Once I delivered the food to the grateful guest, I went back to the front desk and took my seat.

"That's the weirdest so far, I've gotta say," Josh said. "For me, at least. Have you seen any other food that was…"

He couldn't find a word to match his facial expression and I grinned. "I've seen food I probably couldn't identify if there was money on the line," I told him. Josh sighed and shook his head. Whenever it came to the oddities of this hotel, he often lapsed into a thoughtful silence. This one was less thoughtful and more dismissive. Maybe he was stuck imagining what tarantula tasted like.

If you're wondering, I hadn't googled that.

"Oh, did you have anything you wanted me to get you from town tomorrow?" Josh asked.

I made a face. "Nah, I'm fine."

For a week or so, I'd found myself wanting things I couldn't buy without leaving the crossroads, like fast food, and Josh had happily stopped for breakfast from Dunkin' Donuts or McDonalds before coming into work. But then I realized that I was only wanting these things because I couldn't get them myself. I had been here for two years without leaving and it had been fine, just like I'd been fine living in a small town growing up. Between the grocery store, This and That, and ordering things online, I really did have everything I needed.

Josh had asked because tomorrow was Tuesday, which was both his and my day off. Weekends were busiest at the hotel, and often people tacked on a Monday or Friday for a three-day trip, so Tuesdays made the most sense. Usually, I spent that time either in my art room, reading a book, watching a movie, or hanging out with a coworker who was also off the clock.

When I'd started working here as the Manager, Mr. Lucero was adamant that I take Tuesday as a real day off rather than use it as an errand day, since I didn't have a full weekend. If I needed groceries, I let Josh handle things for a bit. The same went for the occasional dentist or doctor appointment at the office complex diagonal to us.

Of course, that was back when I thought I was alive and needed to do that stuff. I still brushed my teeth (if I was capable of making my breath consistently minty fresh, I didn't know how yet) but no more worrying about cholesterol or cavities. Being dead does have its perks.

It was taking a while for me to get comfortable talking about my new state of being. Josh helped immensely, in large part because, until he'd worked here, he often spent his days seeing dead people. And occasionally being pestered by them for help. The crossroads being the odd place that it is, ghosts can't exist here, so he'd told me it was a relief for him to be hired. Even after we found out about me, he didn't seem irritated by it, probably because we'd already become friends by that point. And he noted that I'm far from the kind of dead people he'd dealt with in the past.

Honestly, Josh had been immensely supportive, sometimes prompting me to say what was on my mind if I had the far-off gaze that meant I was thinking about it too hard. We talked about my parents and anyone else who I knew from before I'd died, who weren't allowed to visit the crossroads.

Also, we discussed my future, though not too much of it. Josh pointed out that I shouldn't think about the next hundred years. I wasn't built for it, and I'd probably end up in a puddle of despair if I tried. Instead, I was taking my new life at the same pace as my old one, just with new restrictions in place. Most of our conversations were short and not that deep, though, since I didn't want to risk bursting into tears while I was on shift. We kept to the basics, mostly covering practical questions and issues.

The computer let off the soft alert noise that let me know we'd received an email, and I turned to open it. "Ah, our enigmatic boss has sent us a message."

"You know, I feel like letters from him should come on parchment, in a heavy envelope with a wax seal," Josh said.

"Delivered by an owl?" I asked. "I don't know what takes up his time, but I'm sure he's got better things to do than that sort of pageantry. And for whatever weird reason Hogwarts had an addiction to messenger birds and quills, it apparently doesn't apply to real wizards. I'm glad, because all we need is another layer on this job to make it more difficult."

"Earthquakes that only happen here aren't difficult?" Josh asked with a grin.

I smirked back and turned to the computer, opening up the email and skimming it. "Ah. Okay, so, it looks like we've got some details for that convention coming to town. This Sunday to Saturday, sixteen rooms, sixteen people."

I hadn't been sure what to call occasions where a group of people filled the hotel, to be honest. Convention was what I'd settled on, even though it sort of gave the feeling that there would be booths selling merchandise and lecture halls filled with people listening to a speaker. But the word 'gathering' or 'get together' were both too informal, like they were only visiting for an afternoon of mingling. And 'conference' felt too much like a business term.

"Coming to town?" My coworker leaned forward. "Calling the crossroads a town is a stretch."

Turning to face him, I nodded. "True. But it really is for these purposes, since they stay here. There's a large room over in the office complex to host things like parties and such," I said, in reference to the corner of the intersection diagonal from us. "They make good use of it. And of course, if people are here overnight, everyone's got to sleep somewhere."

Josh glanced at the screen, curious. "What kind of convention is it exactly?" he asked.

"Sometimes we don't know. The guests and their privacy." He nodded knowingly. "I did know that the last one was some sort of inter-species mingle, after a conflict. I wasn't privy to the details of the conflict, of course. But *this* email says everyone's headed here to find a mate."

"What, like speed dating?" he asked, suddenly smiling in amusement.

I chuckled. "A week isn't that speedy, but I guess so. And this calls for a meetup of our own," I said, taking my walkie from my belt. Josh would get the lowdown from the email in a moment, but I'd need to meet with the department heads to discuss what needed to be done. I turned the knob to channel two and asked Fyfe to go to channel three.

"Hey you two," I said. "Got a message from on high about the con starting this Sunday. Meet in the break room during Andrea's dinner break? Over."

Whenever it was time to go over something important, or if one of us just wanted to vent, because we do work in hospitality after all, we'd meet up in the evening. Andrea usually took her dinner break last after everyone else in the diner, so Fyfe and I would come over to the break room after our shifts were over at nine p.m. And sometimes she had treats, as was the case today.

I gasped softly and outstretched my hands, making little grasping motions at the muffins, as I walked over to the table she was sitting at. "Yummies…"

"A guest requested blueberry muffins, and we have leftovers," Andrea said.

Fyfe was already at the table with a muffin on his plate that had a bite taken out of it, looking satisfied. "How you doing, lassie?"

"Good. I had to bring a guest's food out to eat in the lobby because Tolinka was eating tarantulas," I said as I pulled the top off the muffin and took a bite.

Andrea chuckled. "He likes them, but I think he orders them just to mess with me, because they're a challenge to cook."

Fyfe swallowed another bite of his muffin. "Maybe I'm underestimating how tasty those things are, but I fear you're probably right," he noted. "But who am I to deny him the entertainment of challenging our resident chef?" He glanced at me. "Speaking of challenges. You got an email from Lucero?"

I tried to quickly finish the large bite of muffin I'd taken. "I did indeed," I replied. "Seems we're hosting a week-long dating excursion. We've got sixteen guests, all female names. I've been told to put a specific half on the first floor and the other half on the second, though no specific room assignments, so I guess each half are different in some way."

"Butch and femme?" Andrea asked.

I snorted. "As if anything in this hotel would be so simple." The woman grinned knowingly. "Apparently, we got a referral from Isadora, after the last time she stayed here. Remember her?"

Andrea's expression turned skeptical. "The one who you said got a complaint about her music volume? Who got tipped an insulting dollar when she tried to play in the lobby? And then got groped by a diner customer you had to ban?" she asked. "That Isadora? *She* recommended they stay here?"

I waved a hand vaguely in the direction of the hotel. "They'll have the hotel to themselves, so that stuff is less relevant, I guess."

Fyfe shook his head. "Maybe the guests are her people, all keen on music like her," he told me through a mouthful of muffin, "but that's probably only part of it. My guess is she was happy with how you handled things when it came to dealing with local arseholes."

"He's got a point," Andrea noted. "Everyone knows the hotel's a great place to stay, but Isadora got several firsthand examples of you enforcing hospitality and such."

"So, in that case, congrats on getting us a big gig, boss," Fyfe said with a smile. I smiled back appreciatively. "List of special notes?"

"Ah, not a lot. Request to clean the baths daily if they look at all visibly dirty, so I'm guessing they're water folks, maybe bringing their own bath bombs or something." He nodded and I glanced at Andrea. "Also, they're super keen on seafood, so you'll be getting an extra shipment, with some fancy stuff. And by fancy, I mean I didn't recognize a few things on the list."

Her eyebrows went up and she nodded. "Nice. I'll break out all the extra gear I might need, make sure we're ready when they all come down for meals at the same time."

"Sounds good," I said with a nod.

"Are we expecting this to be a mingling sort of event, or should I buy myself some earplugs for later in the week?" Fyfe asked seriously.

"Oh, for fuck's sake!" I laughed. "How the hell should I even know?"

Andrea grinned and leaned forward. "You've said you had interest in girls in the past," she said pointedly.

I rolled my eyes. "I'm picky though, like eighty-twenty."

"And you'll have sixteen to choose from," she told me, with a grand gesture toward the hotel. "It's like your own private version of the bachelorette!"

Fyfe cackled and I shut my eyes briefly and shook my head. "As if any potential dating in my future won't be complicated enough," I groused, "you also want to add in that it's one of our nonlocal guests?"

"Woman's got a point, though," Fyfe said. "It's not as if you're spoiled for options. Plus, she's not saying you should marry one, but at least get laid. How long's it been?"

My eyes bulged out. "I'm not talking about my sex life with you!"

"What sex life?" Andrea shot back.

I couldn't stop myself from bursting out laughing, drawing out a cheeky smile from Fyfe. "Jesus Christ. Why am I the one that's suddenly the target of this conversation?"

"Because my sex life is grand already. Thanks very much for asking," Fyfe replied.

"I did not ask," I said, shaking my head.

Andrea chuckled. "Come on, who are you going to talk to about this stuff besides your best friends? Just cause I'm as old as your mom and Fyfe's as old as your grandpa, you think everything in us got switched off?" She shook her head. "Ain't how it works."

I slumped in my chair, leaning my head back. "Maybe I'll consider it if the occasion…presents itself as an option," I said slowly. "But it honestly hasn't been something that I've been thinking about a whole lot. It feels big."

"I know, dear," Fyfe said, his tone changing to something surprisingly gentle. "We just don't want you falling for the idea that you're destined to be alone." He met my gaze, and I averted my eyes.

"Right." I shook my head, feeling a surge of something swell in my chest. I really didn't want the conversation to devolve into my current issues. "Can we change the subject?"

Andrea obliged me immediately. "Well. Jodie got a sparkly tip today."

I sat up straight, at attention. "That's what I'm talking about! Do tell."

Chapter 2

Of all the curiosities that come from living and working at the crossroads, the inexplicable weather is the oddest. To me, at least. Something about it pouring down rain when the sky is a perfect blue in all directions just seems more unreasonable than strange people or weird happenings here and there.

That Wednesday, I was behind the counter sketching, per usual, though I'd swapped out my customary Ticonderoga #2 for graphite. I've been using my nice graphite pencils a lot these days. Then, the volume of the conversations in the diner rose enough to be noticeable, and the tone was concerned, which pulled my attention away from my art. It was just me, since Josh was on his lunch break. Putting down the sketchpad, I stood up and my attention went to the motion of falling snow visible through the front door and the large glass window.

I sighed. "Ugh, great."

The bizarre weather never lasted long, only a few hours, but it could be a pain in the butt. Not that it stuck around; it was mostly an issue for anyone outside at the moment. As every northerner knows, after you get a few inches of snow, it sucks to get a melt and then a freeze, because then everything's ice. You've got to walk like a penguin or risk slipping and falling hard on your butt. But this was a different situation.

I'd only experienced it once, but we got snow for a few hours, and then it went back to normal. In this case, normal was summer. It wasn't as if Fyfe would have to go out to shovel it; even if we got a decent amount, it wouldn't stick to things because they were still hot from the sun. It melted on contact. The only real problem for me was the guests who freaked out.

Actually, there was also the slipperiness. I grabbed two Wet Floor signs from where they were propped up under the desk. I quickly walked over, and the automatic doors opened to let me put one outside, and I also put one inside, about six feet in. People running from the surprise snowstorm were likely to be thinking of other things besides, 'Oh, the floor might be slippery,' when fleeing for shelter. I brushed away the flakes that had landed on my head and shoulders, walking back behind the desk.

I mostly felt bad for the trees, plants, and smaller animals skittering around the forest. I had this comical image in my head of frantic squirrels terrified that they'd slept through fall and hadn't packed away enough acorns for winter.

My clothes were business casual, but I was still wearing a short-sleeved shirt. This would become relevant because the air conditioning was still going, fighting a never-ending battle against the heat. Taking my walkie from my belt, I flicked to channel two. "Marjorie for Fyfe."

"Go for Fyfe."

I put on the tone of an airline pilot as I spoke, "If you look out the window to our right, you'll see the sky doing a lovely impression of winter."

There was a pause and I guessed he was doing housekeeping in a room with the curtains closed, because a few moments later his irritated voice came over the walkie in reply. "Ah, shite."

The next few hours would necessitate Fyfe playing with the heat/cooling controls like a DJ with a mixing board. He'd need to balance it so that it didn't get too cold inside, but we knew the heat would return, and the last thing we wanted was for the snow to come to an end and suddenly have the heat blasting when it was once again ninety degrees outside.

"What is going on?" asked a panicked voice. A man in his forties speed-walked over to me, and I assumed he hadn't been satisfied with the answer he'd gotten from our servers. "It's *snowing!*"

"Marjorie out," I spoke into the walkie, just in case Fyfe had planned on continuing the conversation. I put the walkie back on my belt to give the customer my full attention. "We get some freaky weather around here sometimes. It never lasts long, maybe a few hours."

"But it was ninety-two when we walked in here," he said, clearly enunciating the words, as if there was something about this that I just wasn't comprehending. "Could this be like that movie, where some flash freeze takes over the planet because of climate change?"

It wasn't the first time a guest had piped up about *The Day After Tomorrow* and it wouldn't be the last. But he looked genuinely freaked out, so I sighed and just let him know my sincere thoughts on that comparison. "We won't be so lucky. Climate change isn't going to hit us in a convenient, two-hour package. It's going to torture us for the next hundred years."

As the man took a moment to process that, Gabriel came out of the diner and walked over to the desk, and I glanced over to him. "Hey. Gonna pull out the winter kit?" I asked knowingly.

"Yup. I helped with the fireplace last winter, so I figured I'd get it going, since Fyfe's busy enough," he told me.

"Appreciate that," I said with a smile. "Thanks, Gabriel."

"Winter kit?" echoed the guest that was still standing there, arms crossed worriedly, as Gabriel made his way to the fireplace.

"When was the last time you roasted marshmallows?" I asked cheerfully.

The winter kit wasn't anything like gloves and jackets. It was Andrea's clever solution to off-season snow. We'd get the fire going in the fireplace in the corner of the lobby, which was closed and cleaned since we hadn't expected to use it until next winter. Andrea would bring out graham crackers, chocolate bars, and marshmallows, and a few dozen skewers. Then the guests could help themselves to the treats once the fire got going.

The front doors opened, and Josh walked in, brushing snow furiously from his clothes and hair. "What the hell?" he cried. He'd decided on cargo shorts that day, with the warm weather and having planned to go out for lunch at the Chinese place, which made me grimace.

"Oh, crap." Looking at the clock, I realized his break had come to an end. "That was bad luck."

Josh rubbed his arms rapidly as he came behind the desk. "For real. My first freaky snowstorm and I get caught in it. Figures."

"This really is normal?" spoke up the guest.

"Normal is a relative word," Josh said with a shrug. "But I heard they break out stuff for s'mores if this happens."

"S'mores?" came an excited cry from the two kids who had come up behind the man. A girl and a boy, who seemed to be about seven and twelve, respectively, suddenly had smiles on their faces. "Dad, can we make s'mores?"

The man finally let his arms relax at his sides, apparently unable to sustain his concern after three employees were undaunted by the snow. "Yeah, of course. We'll finish our lunch first, though. Where's Mom?"

"She won't stop staring out the window," said the boy with a long-suffering sigh. "It's like she thinks the sky is falling."

"It's snowing!" came a shriek from a young voice. I looked behind them and my eyes widened in surprise as Mitzy sprinted into the lobby, her eyes wide.

"Oh my god, why were you out there?" exclaimed the father worriedly, rushing over to take a knee and brush snow off her. His parenting instincts kicked in for the random child. "You must be freezing."

I hadn't expected Mitzy, but to be fair, I never expect her. She's a young girl who makes appearances occasionally, I'd say at least every six months if not more often, to ask if there are any children staying at the hotel. And the man was right; with her shorts, t-shirt, and Crocs, Mitzy was in no way dressed for a snowstorm. Her arms were tightly folded, and she rapidly swept her head back and forth to dislodge the snow from her pigtails.

"Why were you outside?" asked the man's daughter, walking over to the two of them.

Mitzy blinked at them. "Hi."

The girl paused. "Hi," she said with a smile. "They're gonna bring out stuff to make s'mores! Want to join us?"

Looking back and forth from the two kids to the man crouched in front of her, I realized Mitzy had relaxed in a way I'd never seen her before. She was always on a mission, needing to ask her questions incessantly about other children. And now, here they were. They weren't guests at the hotel, but they were customers at the diner, and they were of course treated as guests in the ways that mattered.

"Do you want a blanket?" I found myself blurting out.

Mitzy's gaze met mine and for once, she smiled, looking just like a ten-year-old girl should. The formality that was so familiar to me was gone, and weirdly, there was also no hint in her eyes that she knew who I was. She was just a little girl looking at me with her light brown eyes. And dimples. I'd never noticed she had *dimples*. "It's okay, I'm fine," she said warmly.

"All right," the man sighed, pushing himself to his feet with a grunt. "Back to the table. Let's see if we can finish our meals before we spot chocolate and marshmallows." He held out a hand and Mitzy took it before turning to guide them all toward the restaurant.

Staring in shock, I watched the four of them start walking and suddenly spoke, "Wait!"

They stopped and looked back toward me expectantly. "Yes?" the father prompted.

I pointed at Mitzy. "She's…going with you?"

"Oh, she's mine too," he replied with a grin. "I just didn't notice she'd slipped outside."

"She…" I looked down to Mitzy and then to the other two children, then back to him, nonplussed. "Are you staying at the hotel?" I managed to ask.

"Oh no, we just stopped for lunch," he told me. "We're taking a trip to see their grandparents."

Nodding, I stared, but as much as I was compelled to continue asking questions, I couldn't figure out anything else to say. They went off to the diner and I looked at Josh. "What just happened?"

He stared after them. "I think Mitzy just…adopted a family?"

Shaking my head, I walked out from behind the counter and over to the diner, stopping at the threshold. The family sat back down at the table, and to my utter shock, there was a plate of mac and cheese there for Mitzy. "What the fuck?" I breathed.

Jodie noticed me and came over, taking note of my expression. "What's wrong?"

"Mitzy…is sitting at that table," I said. "And that man just said she's his daughter."

The woman's eyes widened, and her gaze shot over to them. "Uh…that's…something. Wait, that's my table, and I didn't bring out that mac and cheese."

"I got it, go ahead," I said dismissively, knowing she had work to do. She nodded and walked off as I considered what to do. Mitzy wasn't a guest. Customers *were*. So, it was my responsibility to keep them safe.

Taking a deep breath, I took my walkie from my belt and flicked to channel two. I figured he was the best to call a coworker before resorting to calling Mr. Lucero. Besides, we had time since they planned to stay for s'mores. "Marjorie for Fyfe."

"Go for Fyfe."

"I've got a, uh…situation. Important and…mildly urgent. Can you come to the diner? Over."

A minute later, Fyfe was standing beside me and looking shocked. "Bloody hell," he muttered. "There is never gonna come a day when I think I've got a handle on this place."

"Do you know anything about her?" I asked. "Patricia said she'd been coming here for…twelve years now, I think?"

"That's right," he said, nodding and looking at me. "Thing is, I had occasion to bring it up to Mr. Lucero once, and he wasn't worried. Never told me what she is, but…" Fyfe squinted, recalling the memory. "He said…she'd keep asking for other kids until she found what she was looking for. I figured that meant she'd never stop, since she would never get what she wanted, but maybe I was wrong."

My lips parted in surprise, and I looked back to Mitzy. The woman at the table said something that made the girl laugh, and I let out a sharp breath. She looked *happy*. She looked like this had always been her family, the way she talked back and forth to the other girl, the way she rolled her eyes at the man who was apparently now her father.

I let out a ragged breath as stress settled on my shoulders. "I need to call the boss. Make sure this is on the up and up."

"I agree, lass," he said, his eyes still on the girl. "Safety first."

Flicking to channel four on the walkie, I tensed before speaking, "Marjorie for Mr. Lucero."

A few seconds passed before he replied. "Go for Lucero."

"Mitzy seems to have…found a family," I said carefully. "And I'm concerned for the safety of our guests. Over."

There was a brief pause before his voice came over the walkie again. To my surprise, there was an audible smile in his tone. "That's wonderful news, Marjorie. As far as we're concerned, she walked in here with them. Over."

Standing statue-still in astonishment as I continued to stare at the family, I gathered my thoughts. "Okay," I finally said. "Marjorie out."

Lowering the walkie to my side, I glanced over at Fyfe. "This hotel, I swear to god." He barked out a laugh and grinned at me, seeming to take great pleasure in my confusion. "Why didn't he just tell me this could happen?"

"Nah, that's not how this works. You know that," he replied. He shook his head. "All the folks we meet keep secrets for good reason, and anything of this sort is need-to-know for us locals. Also…" He looked back at Mitzy. "As far as we know, she *was* dangerous. Until…she wasn't."

Chapter 3

You never know what a day will bring, and so my mornings can be a strange contrast since they all start off so normally, with the same routine. Unless I was woken mid-sleep of course, for some emergency, which does happen on occasion. When I first wake up and shut off the alarm on my phone, I'll splash some water on my face before tiredly walking into the kitchen to turn on my coffee maker. The coffee in the lobby is great, but I prefer to have a cup when I first wake up, so I'm not subjected to questions from the guests while caffeine deprived.

I have breakfast, then brush my teeth and get dressed. Then I'll give a once-over to the app on my phone that connects to the hotel's software, so I can see what's going on. For instance, this morning, the front desk had received a call at a quarter after eight about problems with the tub in room six. Also, I'll read any notes from overnight, from both the front desk and housekeeping, otherwise known as Carl and Paul, respectively.

By that time, I feel sufficiently awake, and I decide what drawing implements I'll be bringing with me to the reception desk as my main way to pass the time. As I mentioned, graphite pencils have been my go-to recently. I've got some cool felt tip pens and markers to play with on occasion, so if I decide to use those, I'll stick them in the pocket of my slacks before heading downstairs.

Today was typical right up until I received a call over the walkie from Fyfe, shortly after I'd gotten to the front desk. "Marj, need you in room six. Important, urgent." His voice was tight and filled with aggravation but didn't sound panicked. Just weary.

That worried me, because a tub having problems when we had an incoming slew of folks fond of bathing could be a real issue. The note in my app said that the guest in room six had been using it this morning when it started clogging up, and by the time she got out, there was a green tint to the water pooled near the drain.

I'd assumed it was backed up; I always assume a mundane explanation until a more unusual one jumped out to startle me. But now, from the tone of Fyfe's voice, it seemed this one was likely to be trouble.

I got up from my chair and speed-walked down the hall. My master key let me into room six, and I shut the door behind me, but only made it a few feet before stopping.

"Oh, not again!" I whined.

There was a frog perched on one of the double beds. The last time this had happened, they'd appeared in a hallway closet, and we couldn't find the source. Luckily the entrance had only let them through for a short time, so that had resolved itself. It had just left me and Fyfe trying to grab a couple dozen frogs who must have been baffled as to where their pond had gone and why their world had gone from wide open space to constrained rectangular spaces with giants wandering about.

And also, of course, they were not happy that the giants were chasing them, expressing their fear and displeasure by pooping.

"My thoughts exactly!" called Fyfe from the bathroom in reply. The door was closed, presumably to keep the frogs inside from escaping. "Listen, just get hold of the one that got out and stuff him in a drawer or something. I've got the rest of them contained in here. Get the net and a container and we'll try to get you in here without letting any out."

"How many are there?"

He paused. "About as bad as last time."

I let out a groan as I slowly made my way toward the frog on the bed. "Hey, buddy," I said softly. "Just stay…right there."

The mistake I'd made often the first time was trying to outdo their speed, which wasn't in my repertoire of skills. All it made for was an exasperating experience. This one hopped once and I kept my movements slow before getting close enough to close my hands around it. At that point, it did fumble a bit in a panic, but I just walked over to the dresser and opened a drawer with my foot, checking it was empty, before putting him in and shutting it.

Brushing off my hands, I let Fyfe know where I'd stored the little fella before I went back out into the hall and over to the second-nearest storage closet, where we kept a large net. The first time, we'd had to go down to the basement to fetch one, and I figured it best just to keep one on hand. I also took a container to store the little buggers in, carrying it by the handle on top.

Then I headed back to the front desk with a benign smile on my face.

Holding out the net and container to Josh, I told him, "Room six has a frog problem in the bathroom. Time for a learning experience."

Even though I'm his boss, Josh and I are friends. So, he did grimace and look warily at the frog-hunting gear. "Don't you have more experience from last time?"

"Yes. Don't try to be faster; they'll show you you're not," I said, taking a step forward to bring them within grasping reach.

He stood up and took them. "Shame on you, pawning this off on a subordinate."

"Guilty as charged. Hey, at least this time they're trapped in the bathroom."

Josh grunted as he walked off and I shook my head, taking a few squirts from the hand sanitizer on the desk and thoroughly cleaning off any frog germs.

For all I knew, the guests arriving soon would be thrilled with the ambience of frogs hopping around, but even if that were so, the hotel is not a wildlife park. The room was currently occupied, and this had to be remedied. So, I went into the section of the computer program I used for maintenance requests and updates and added to the list, 'snake and Drain-o all tubs to ensure no buildup.'

There was no way to fully avoid a sudden appearance of frogs, but the least we could do was make sure there weren't any hiding in wait.

When all the frogs had been caught (and Josh had thoroughly washed his hands and changed into a spare shirt from his break room locker that didn't have poop on it), he sat back down at the desk with a ragged sigh. "I saw the update. When you say you want Fyfe to *snake* the drains…"

I grinned. "Once again…not Hogwarts."

Josh snorted. "Just feels like it sometimes." He nodded toward my sketchpad. "Another photo today?"

"Yeah, this is Paul Cadden," I replied. I tapped the picture I'd printed out. "I found it on Pinterest and thought it'd be awesome to draw. He does really cool things with perspective."

"I can see that," Josh noted. "Can't wait to see the finished product."

Later that afternoon, not long after I got back from my lunch break at the diner, two kids came up to the front desk, and one of them piped up, "Excuse me."

Josh and I both turned our attention to them, and I put aside my sketchpad, pushing myself to my feet since only the top of the girl's head was visible. They were an older sister and younger brother, I'd guess they were eleven and eight years old respectively, and they'd checked in with their father. He'd left this morning with a briefcase, wearing a suit, and so my first thoughts were of concern.

"How can I help you?" I asked.

They both had a guilty, worried look on their faces. "Dad said we were absolutely, positively not supposed to leave the room unless we were bleeding or the hotel was on fire," the girl explained as a preamble.

"Is there blood or fire?" I asked.

"No-no-no, it's fine," she said, waving her hands quickly. "We just… Well…we were playing…and we lost my dad's sunglasses. They're his favorite and I think they're expensive."

"All right," I coaxed. There was definitely more to this story.

The little brother nudged her. "Tell her!" he whispered.

"You put them in!"

"It was an accident!"

"You're still in trouble!"

I waited patiently, eyebrows raised.

"Okay, so…it's really weird," the girl told me.

I smiled comfortingly. "That's fine. Weird tends to be a specialty of mine." I pointed to my name tag. "I'm the Manager here. My name's Marjorie."

"I'm Patty. This is George," the girl told me. "So…there's this hole in the air…in our room…and if you drop things into it, they disappear. *Like magic.* I promise I'm not lying." Her tone was earnest and determined, which was objectively adorable, considering the past two years of my life here.

My eyes narrowed in concern. "How big is the hole?" was my first question.

"Liiiike that big," Patty said, holding her hands about six inches apart.

At that, my worry tempered a bit. When I'd been hired, I'd been told that guests have never gone missing, and I'd never heard of something like this, but I'd only been here two years. "How about you show me?" I asked, taking a few steps backwards. I gave Josh a nod, which he returned, a wordless transfer of front desk duties, as I walked out from behind the desk.

Following the kids, they led me to room two, just around the corner. Patty gasped in dismay. "I forgot the key card!"

Karen Avizur

"Lucky you've got the Manager with you, then," I said with an amused smile, pulling the master key from its retractable loop around my belt. She ducked her head sheepishly. Opening the door, I held it for them and then let it shut behind us.

"It's over here," Patty said, walking to the bed. "Oh, this is a washable marker, I promise!"

I noticed a green X near the center of one of the two double beds, which had been made this morning. "I appreciate that, but it's not my biggest concern at the moment. Anyway, I once had a kid find a package of colorful Sharpies in their parent's bag and draw a mural across the wall," I replied, examining the room attentively. I saw some coloring books and two board games, as well as the expected personal belongings here and there, but room service had come through, so it was quite tidy.

Gesturing to the X, I asked, "Is that where the hole is?"

"Oh no, it's up here," George spoke up, climbing onto the bed. His older sister did so as well. He stepped up to the X and waved his hand up and down a little, which alarmed me until he said, "But I can't put my finger through or anything. You gotta drop little things in, like this." He pretended to have something in his hand and let it fall.

"How did you *find* it?" I asked incredulously. My tone was borderline impressed.

At this point it seemed the kids were satisfied I was taking them seriously, as they were becoming less nervous. "We were throwing Goldfish up in the air to catch them in our mouths," Patty replied. "But I didn't want to do it on the floor, because it's dirty and we're not good at catching them so we have to pick them back up, and the sheets are washed every day."

"Smart," I remarked.

Patty nodded. "And then I threw one up and…it didn't come down. It just disappeared."

"And we did it again and again, it was so funny," George said, smiling despite himself. "And then-"

"Then you started to drop other stuff in," I said with a tired smile. "Alright, here." I went into my pocket and took out one of the dime-a-dozen pens I carried with me, holding it out to Patty. "Can I get a demonstration?"

She took it and stood next to the X, appearing to do some mental calculations against her height, and then held up the pen. After a brief moment of setting her aim, she dropped it. And sure enough, after about a foot, it vanished into thin air.

Even if these portals were everywhere, it'd be ridiculous to try to find any, I mused. Unless they were only a foot off the floor and someone happened to drop something, it was unlikely anyone would discover one. This was quite a funny anomaly.

That had been my primary worry when it came down to it, whether there were more of these. Fyfe had briefly made an involuntary trip to a neighboring dimension recently, but he was there less than a minute before he returned. And that was because of growing pains in the hotel, which had passed, so it wasn't a general concern. But the items that had been vanishing were going somewhere, and I had no idea where they were ending up. It could be that there was a small pile of Goldfish and other detritus, including a pair of sunglasses, in the basement. Or it could be some fae dimension.

It felt like overkill to call in my boss for this. Mr. Lucero was a stunningly powerful wizard, and this was definitely crossroads magic, but it still felt like killing a mosquito with a sledgehammer. Nonetheless, I couldn't very well take care of it on my own. It was definitely outside my wheelhouse.

Taking my walkie from my side, I flicked to channel four. "Marjorie for Mr. Lucero."

There was a brief pause. "Go for Lucero."

"Can I see you in room two, please? We have a small issue. Over." I figured there was no need to get him worried unnecessarily.

"On my way. Lucero out." I clipped the walkie back to my belt.

"Who was that?" George asked.

"That was *my* boss," I told him. "He'll know what to do because this is his hotel. He's owned it for a long time." It was prudent of me, I think, to not tell them that in this case, a long time was over a hundred and fifty years.

We didn't have to wait long before I heard the sound of a key in the door, and it swung open. Despite his actual age, my boss appeared to be in his late fifties or early sixties, with graying dark brown hair and a goatee. I'd yet to see him wearing anything other than a suit. He walked over to my side, curiously surveying the scene, including the children and the X marked on the bed. "What seems to be the issue?"

I took another pen from my pocket. "George. Care to do the honors?"

The young boy took a few steps toward me on the bed to take the pen, then went over to the X, lifted the pen, and dropped it.

"Ah," my boss muttered. "Goodness."

I explained the method by which they'd manage to locate it. "Then they got to having fun, and tossed a few other things in there too. Including their dad's sunglasses. Then they realized they may have miscalculated."

An amused smile spread across his face. "I see. Well, you two are impressive," Mr. Lucero spoke, glancing at the children. He slipped off his loafers, stepping up onto the bed. "These are very rare, but my grandmother told me about them. They're flat and small, so they're called freckle portals."

"Portals?" Patty asked, her eyes widening. "To where?"

"I'm not sure." He reached into his pocket and took out a small Ziploc bag. "This is salt. Here, look."

Opening it up, he tipped it and let a little river start sliding into the hole, a bizarre sight as it disappeared from view. They kids watched with wide eyes, riveted, and gasped as things started flying out of the hole, like they were being thrown back, and falling to the bed. There were a handful of Goldfish, a crumpled-up piece of paper, several Crayons, and the sunglasses.

"Salt is used for all sorts of things with magic, and strange things don't like it," he remarked as he picked up one of the Goldfish. Dropping it where the portal had been, it fell straight down to the bed.

"It's gone!" Patty exclaimed. She and George both tested that several times, but it had indeed vanished.

Mr. Lucero stepped off the bed and slid back into his loafers. "Thank you for telling an adult so we could take care of it. That was responsible of you," he told them. "I must get back to work, but it was nice to meet you."

"You too," said Patty distractedly, looking at where the portal had been.

I followed my boss out of the room, letting the door shut behind us. We walked a few yards down the hall, in the direction of his apartment, before I asked quietly, "Freckle portals?"

"Seemed an appropriate name," he said with a small smile. "And there won't be anything on the internet about them."

"And they'll never find one again anyway. Was the salt actually necessary? As an add-on I mean, while you closed it with your *left hand*?"

Mr. Lucero's smile widened, and he slowed to a stop, meeting my gaze. "You noticed."

"I'm pretty sure this was the first time I've ever seen sleight-of-hand used to distract from the use of actual magic," I remarked. "So, do you *need* to do some motion with your hand to direct your magic?"

He moved his head back and forth. "I don't exactly need to. But…a friend from Europe likened doing magic while remaining still to someone from Italy speaking without moving their hands."

I let out a sudden laugh. "Gotcha. So, these portals. Are they rare?"

He nodded once. "They are. And the salt was to distract them, but educational, nonetheless. There are many instances where salt is used protectively in magic." He took a breath and turned thoughtful. "Considering the frogs you caught this morning in addition to this, I'll move up my schedule and direct some more power into the wards that keep these kinds of things from opening. This might just be a glitch, or indeed it might have been there for years without us noticing, but better to be on the safe side."

I nodded slowly. "True. Hey, can I ask you something?" He raised his eyebrows upwards in inquiry.

Lately I've been asking more questions than I had for the first two years or so. I'd always taken the attitude that there were important things I needed to know, so I shouldn't borrow trouble by asking for background on every strange thing I noticed. But once I'd found out I'd be spending the rest of my 'life' here, I was struck with a newfound curiosity and the urge to know more. And surprisingly, Mr. Lucero hadn't been hesitant at all in answering my questions, even if the answer was, occasionally, that he couldn't tell me.

I gave him an expressive look. "Whenever I call you, it doesn't take long at all for you to arrive, no matter where I am. You're only past the hotel's rooms," I said with a gesture toward the stairwell that had a door to his building, "but…it always feels like it should take a little longer. Is there a shortcut available?"

Mr. Lucero chuckled. "For you? No. And it takes a wizard about sixty to eighty years to become proficient."

At that, he took a couple of steps toward room seven, turned the doorknob without the keycard, and he pushed the door open to reveal his office, letting it gradually shut behind him. After staring for a long moment, I slid in my master keycard and the mechanism beeped and unlocked. I opened the door, revealing room seven, clean and ready for its next guest.

Karen Avizur

Chapter 4

The day before guests were set to arrive and fill up the hotel for the convention, Josh and I were at the front desk putting flower arrangements in vases, following instructions we'd gotten by email. This specific room décor had been requested by Mr. Lucero, not the guests, though some people did often ask for add-ons like this. Since Fyfe still had his regular daily to-do list, which kept him busy, we were trying to help whenever possible in preparation for the influx.

Our boss was the one who knew details about the guests that we weren't privy to, so he'd make these kinds of decisions, and I knew this would be a nice surprise when they arrived. There were always clues, and Josh was surprisingly good at guessing who or what they were, which he ascribed to the extensive amount of fantasy books he'd read years back. But usually, he kept his thoughts to himself. The guests did prefer the illusion of secrecy even if employees had some accurate guesses. When they were only here for a few days, and sometimes we didn't even get their surnames, discretion was just more polite.

Nancy brought us the materials we needed, but like anything complex that came from the never-ending magical source of Storage, it needed to be 'assembled' by us. You couldn't ask Nancy for a specific flower arrangement, even if you printed it out and gave it to her. But she retrieved everything we needed, which on top of the vases included freshly cut lavender, sea thrift, day lily, and a bunch of artemisia to balance everything in a bouquet of green.

We found instructions online to keep the flowers fresh as long as possible, just as you would do if you received a delivery of flowers as a gift. Seven days was a long time to keep them looking freshly picked, and you'll be amused to know that a small sprinkle of Viagra was included in the water. It's common knowledge that the internet has a wide range of curious, made-up tips on a wide spectrum of topics, but this was one that had scientifically been found to be true.

The comedic irony in the fact that we were putting it in bouquets for an all-female dating week did not escape me.

Josh and I were finishing the ninth and tenth vases, the gentle scent of flowers drifting around the reception desk, when I heard Nancy call over to me. Her tone was mildly alarmed. "Uh, Marjorie?"

I put down the flowers in my hand and stood up, walking out from behind the desk and my eyes widened. "Puppy," I said instinctively, my voice going up several octaves.

"Sorry, what?" Josh asked. I heard him get up from his seat.

There was nothing more to add. There was a puppy, in the back of the lobby.

It was completely black with a fluffy coat and looked maybe two months old, and it was *adorable*. It seemed to have wandered out from the hall leading to the rooms, but we were pet friendly, so there was no real reason for one of the guests to sneak it in. Though they could have been trying to save money and dodge the pet fee, or worried we would turn them away since one this young wouldn't be housebroken yet. But something about it led me to believe it had gotten in here another way.

"Hello," I spoke up with a smile.

It was always a risk to assume something was an animal, when in fact it could be a guest, so I didn't immediately crouch and make cooing noises. But its demeanor quickly made me think it was indeed just what it appeared to be, with the uncertain gait of a puppy who had not yet mastered walking. Its tail was down between its legs, its ears were back, and its eyes looked around with a wariness that pulled at my heartstrings.

"Marjorie, are you sure…" Josh's worried voice trailed off. His concern was quite fair, and completely expected, because his first encounter with something *other* was a giant, bloodied wolf that had walked through the front door and checked in as a guest.

"Oh, this is definitely a puppy," I said, my voice only just loud enough for him to hear, before slowly walking forward.

The little cutie's nose was going like crazy to vacuum up smells, and it looked nervous about the results of the analysis that its brain was reporting back. Clearly it was clueless as to what was going on and had not meant to pay us a visit. At that point, it let out an apprehensive whimper. "Hey, it's okay," I said, crouching to make myself seem smaller. "You're safe here. We'll find out where you're supposed to be."

Holding out my hand, the puppy slowly and warily waddled toward me until it managed to sniff me, and I let it do so for a moment before carefully giving it scritches under its chin. "There we go. You're okay." Lowering myself to one knee, I continued to pat it gently and the puppy moved a little closer, giving me a more thorough sniffing. Then, very carefully, I picked it up under its stomach, supporting it under its bottom.

Giving a quick glance to its underside, I said, "Our visitor is a little girl," and then let her snuggle into my arms. I noticed she had dirt on her paws and between her toes, which made it clear she wasn't a dog that spent all her time indoors. For all I know, and it was likely considering how confused she seemed at what she'd encountered here, she lived outside. I was just lucky that she was young enough to trust a random massive creature she'd likely never seen before.

"Let me take a look at her," Nancy spoke up. I walked over and she let the puppy sniff her hand as she gave it a once-over. "Yeah, this thick fur, those paws? She's gonna be big." She looked up to me anxiously. "Real big."

"Well, it's not like I'm keeping her," I said with a smirk.

Nancy gave me a look. "I'm more worried about the ones who are fully grown that are looking for her."

I blinked. "Ah. That's a good point." With a grimace, I looked around. "I mean we recently had frogs again; things come through on occasion. Mr. Lucero took them and…did whatever it is he does to get them back to where they belonged. I'm guessing it's the same case here." As much as they had looked like normal frogs, they definitely hadn't been from around these parts. And I was pretty sure that otherworldly invasive frogs would have some downsides.

Glancing down to the puppy's mushy face, I winced in concern. Earth's dogs had litters, and while a friend of mine had a dog who only had three, some birthed over a dozen puppies. It could be that this one could be an only child, but I considered it unlikely. So, when you had a bunch of kids, how long would it take to realize one was missing? Even more than that, were we about to be overrun? Were the siblings about to find the same entry point and follow?

"Want me to email the boss?" she asked. "We'll look after her until he has time to figure this out."

Movement caught my eye to my right, and I blinked, trying to clear a blurry spot in my vision. I realized quickly that it was not something I could clear away, however. And my heart skipped a beat as I saw that Nancy's train of thought had been right on the money. Whether this was Mama or Papa, they were *big*.

A huge black dog came walking into the hall out of nowhere, moving determinedly, and I could hear its nose snuffling deeply as it followed the trail of its pup. It was clearly the parent, a fully grown version of this puppy, with smooth, thick black fur covering its body. Then it froze, setting its eyes on me.

"Hi," I croaked.

It growled, a sound I felt through the sole of my shoes, and the exhale brought smoke with it.

At least I knew my headstone wouldn't read, '*Died because she couldn't resist a cute puppy*,' since it was already in a graveyard somewhere with my body. But a bite from this dog would still be staggeringly painful. From its size, I wouldn't be surprised if its jaw could clamp down on my leg and shatter bones, and it didn't matter if I could heal any wound. That would not be a pleasant experience.

Swallowing hard, I began to crouch down very slowly. "Welcome to the Crossroads Hotel," I said quietly. "I assume this is your daughter. We were worried for her safety and I'm glad to see you were able to follow her trail."

The puppy had noticed the presence of her parent and perked up, happily leaving my arms and bouncing down the hall, ears flapping. As soon as she was within reach, the parent thoroughly sniffed her, then licked her repeatedly. After that, it chuffed angrily in the puppy's face, and from the body language, it was clear to me the little girl knew her adventure had not been parent-approved.

Looking up to me, the giant dog's body language had relaxed, and it glanced around for a moment, surveying its surroundings. I wasn't sure of its intelligence level, but it was clearly quite high. Understanding gleamed in its eyes and it let out a long breath, this time without a waft of smoke, before leaning down and picking up the puppy by the scruff of her neck. Then it turned and wandered off back the way it had come, disappearing through the same invisible door.

I pushed myself back to my feet and sighed. Then I looked to Nancy, who was visibly relieved. "She was so cute," I pouted. "I wish she could've stayed longer."

"For those of us who aren't effectively immortal, I'll just say that I'm glad that went as smoothly as it did," Nancy said, her voice tight as she glared at me.

Smiling, I shrugged. "Yeah, that's fair." I paused, looking at the door to Storage, and my eyes widened. "Could we-"

She promptly told me, "I can't put things back. Any puppy that comes out of that door is here to stay." After a beat, her expression softened. "But hey, I'm sure we could ask around, find a puppy to come visit you on your day off."

"I'm not, like, a huge dog person, but…" I gave her a plaintive look. "Sometimes you just want to snuggle with a puppy."

Nancy gave me a grin. "I can't argue with you on that."

"Hey," Josh said indignantly, leaning over the top of the counter as I walked back. "What just happened? How come I didn't get to pat the puppy?"

"Because one of her parents showed up and it could've taken down a lion," I told him.

Josh straightened, grunted, and said, "Fair enough."

We continued with our floral work, stopping whenever a guest approached the front desk needing assistance or the phone rang. Josh and I eventually finished the flower arrangements and lined them up out of the way at the end of the counter, in rows of two. Fyfe had turned over the rooms by then, so he came by shortly after to take them two at a time and distribute them.

Once Josh headed out at the end of his shift at 5 p.m., swapping with Delilah whose shift went until 1 a.m., people started coming in for dinner. Since we are out of the way, the diner doesn't get stuffed full of customers for what I call the 'dinner rush', but it was Saturday and we do have seriously good food. They were kept pretty busy. Most of the customers had trickled out as we got toward the end of my shift though. My mind was on the guests who would be arriving the next day, and I assumed, quite wrongly, that my day was pretty much over.

It was not over. We got robbed.

We're in the middle of nowhere, so it's not that surprising when someone targets the crossroads, but it's usually not the hotel. The robbers have to keep an eye on both the front desk and the diner, which is tricky. Plus, it can often be a crapshoot how much money is in a hotel drawer. So, if something happens, it's generally a shop in the plaza across the street that gets hit.

That's not to say we don't have standard security measures in place. After 9 p.m., guests can only come in and out of the hotel with their room key. There are cameras covering all the important spots, including the front desk and the checkout counter in the diner. Mr. Lucero and I both have access to the system, though, in case we need to delete footage that we can't risk being seen by someone local. He goes through it every night to check.

The fact that I work at *this* hotel might make you less concerned. You might have an image of a dozen nonlocals seeing someone come into the diner to rob it and all slowly standing up in unison and proceed to make the robber wish they'd never been born. But all nonlocals know even if they might be nigh invulnerable, all humans are fragile.

As the Manager, anyone here will let me take the lead, and they will also follow all instructions from other employees. And Mr. Lucero's policy is clear: Our lives are worth more than the register. More than the sum of an entire year's worth of gold and gemstone tips, he'd told me firmly. Standing orders are to graciously hand it all over.

That being said…well. My guess is that this isn't a place they'd rob if they knew who frequented it and who owned it.

There were two of them, both male and wearing ski masks, and both had a drawstring bag in one hand and a gun in the other. That combined with the fact that they split up without hesitation and were promptly barking their commands made me think this wasn't the first time they'd done this.

"Let me see your hands! Now!" yelled the one walking toward me. "Stand up."

I'd already leaned forward to stand, the movement disguising my finger hitting one of the panic buttons under the desk, and I raised both hands in the air. Mr. Lucero would be alerted and check the cameras so he could follow what was happening.

"All right. Everything's yours," I said with a calm that I didn't feel, avoiding eye contact and staring at his chest deferentially.

My heart beat thunderously in my chest. I'd been wondering if knowing I was dead would help dampen fear in dangerous situations, but it turns out that kind of stuff is embedded deep in our brains. In my peripheral vision, I saw Delilah also following his orders, her hands trembling. I'd moved a little to my left as I got up and she moved to her right, whether consciously or unconsciously, as I spoke up and took charge.

Did I want to get shot? Fuck no, it would still be agony. And a headshot would be a goddamn mess. Would I get shot to make sure it wasn't Delilah? Absolutely. I'd do it for any of the employees there. As far as I knew, none of the other employees could heal so much as a hangnail.

"Open the register, everything in the bag." He put the bag on the counter, gun pointed straight at me.

Staring down the barrel actually made my vision blur a little. Taking a slow breath to try and calm my racing heart, I told him, "I've got to hit two buttons to open it."

"Do it."

I did, and the register slid open. I quickly took out the pile of cash for each denomination. Then I put it all in the bag. After that, without him asking, I lifted the tray and put it aside, revealing a few larger bills, and he was close enough to watch as I rapidly gathered them all together and shoved them into the bag as well.

"Good. Now the safe."

I didn't hesitate, but that angered me. It meant a former guest was in on this. They must have seen an employee drop one of their tips into the safe under the front desk or the one behind the dining room checkout counter, or both. It was the only way this guy could have known about them. I know, our local guests are all just people, but it still felt like a betrayal.

Punching in the combo for the small safe, I reached in and detached the cloth bag that caught the tips and showed him the contents. He gave a sharp nod, and I put it in his bag as well. With that, he gathered both sides of the drawstring with one hand and pulled the bag to his side, jolting it a few times to partially close it while still holding a gun on me.

At that, he patiently waited for his partner. It's not surprising he was taking longer; even though plenty of people checked in with cash, the diner did many more transactions than the front desk. And they had more opportunities for tips.

But it wasn't long before his buddy shouted for everyone to stay where they were until they were gone, and he ran out of the diner. Then they were both bolting out the front doors, to their waiting car, I assumed.

Letting out a long, shuddering breath, I lowered my arms and turned to Delilah. "Hey, you okay?" I asked her as I took out my walkie, flicking to channel four. I noticed my hands were trembling, and it was more difficult to work my fingers than usual. Trying to push aside my feelings for just a few more moments, I took another slow breath.

"Yeah, I'm good," she said quietly, slowly lowering her arms to her sides. She went back to her chair and sank into it, looking shaken, and I heard a car take off at a speed that would leave skid marks.

"Marjorie for Lucero," I spoke, walking out from behind the desk.

There was barely a pause. "Go."

"We're good here at the front desk," I said, speed-walking into the diner. "No shots fired. Diner looks good too." I saw unsteady but composed employees, two of whom were comforting the only two customers they had.

That's when I heard a faint screech of a car swerving back and forth and then the unmistakable sound of it crashing from flipping over.

My eyes looked in the direction of the front doors, and then I darted over to them, staring out past the floodlights into the dark night. I stood there motionless for a moment. "What was that?" I spoke into the walkie.

"It seems they were overeager in their getaway," my boss said coolly. "I'm outside my back door and can see the car clearly from here. Even if they're still alive, I'm sure they're unconscious. Over."

A small, wan smile appeared on my face. "How unfortunate… Are the police on their way? Over."

"They are. I gave them a thorough description of what was happening, and they should be here soon. I locked down the hotel once the robbers had left, and I'll unlock it when the police arrive on the property. Please extend some comforting hospitality to our guests in the diner. Over."

"Will do, boss. Marjorie out." I lowered my walkie to my side, letting out a sigh, and clipped it to my belt. Noticing my hands were still shaking, I leaned back against the wall, slowly breathing in and out as the adrenaline flushed through my system.

Flipped their car... I smiled spitefully. *What horrible luck.*

Chapter 5

The police arrived shortly, with two ambulances and a fire truck close behind them. They took everyone's statements as the robbers were carted off, and let us know we'd get the cash and jewels back eventually, but they were taken in as evidence for now. The men were both injured and unconscious when they were found in the car but gradually became more alert shortly after they were extracted by the medics.

Once we'd put up the Closed sign for the diner, Andrea pulled out several flavors of ice cream and various toppings. I came down from my apartment to get a bowl of vanilla with chocolate sauce and sprinkles, joining my coworkers in the break room. We were all tired from the stress, and mostly ate our comfort food in silence. I brought a bowl of chocolate chunk to reception for Delilah too, of course. Paul was hanging out with her, and I expected he'd do so for most of the night. Neither of them wanted to spend their shift alone, and luckily there wasn't much to be done, since we had no guests and were fully prepped for the next day.

It took me longer than usual to fall asleep, my mind replaying what had happened, except it kept thinking of all the things that could've gone horribly wrong.

Unsurprisingly, I did have a nightmare. The weird part was that it didn't involve the robbery. I was trying to do my job, but everyone kept complaining I didn't look right, and I realized I was disappearing. Frantic that I was going to vanish, I painted myself with everything I had, going through tubes of paint one after another, so people would still be able to see me. Since this was a dream, calm solutions went out the window, and instead of going to Mr. Lucero to ask for help, I just remained drenched in terror, convinced I was dissolving into nothing.

I woke up with my heart racing and tears in my eyes. Turning on my bedside light, I rubbed my face and wiped away the tears, then wrapped my arms around myself and breathed deeply.

Weirdly, from day one, I didn't feel like the 'I should be a ghost' idea of being dead bothered me. I could heal a stubbed toe or a papercut, but the aggravating pain still always happened, so it's not like I felt dead. If anything, I thought maybe I'd *never* disappear, stuck here forever even if I wanted to move onto the afterlife, whatever it entailed, after a hundred years. But unfortunately, dreams aren't meant to make sense and bring some brilliant clarity to your life. Mostly they're just shitty and annoying.

After making myself a comforting cup of instant hot cocoa, I went back to bed, and it didn't take me that long to fall back to sleep.

The next morning, once I was fully caffeinated and had gone to the diner for breakfast, I went to the front desk to go through everything on my morning checklist. I'd been told our guests wouldn't be arriving until that afternoon, and that was accurate. The first women walked in a little after one o'clock.

The four of them all looked in their late twenties or early thirties, though they were of various ethnicities, and were each wearing some variety of linen tunic dress. Also, each of them had an instrument with them. Three had what I could only guess was a lyre, each looking particularly well-crafted, and one had a flute.

One of them stepped forward, a woman with long, wavy brown hair who introduced herself as Raidne, to let me know it was her car they'd arrived in. "Not all of us have cars, so we carpooled," she explained. "I was told it was recommended to have a vehicle, in case we'd like to leave the crossroads and hike to rivers or swimming holes."

I nodded. "There's the swimming hole in the forest a mile or so southwest of the auto shop, and that's the one most of our guests visit. I've been to it only twice, but it's beautiful. It's difficult to get to, though, so most locals don't bother, which can be an upside. But yes, there are other spots within driving distance that I've heard are wonderful."

Even though it was so far away, the swimming hole, and indeed the forest that surrounded the area, was Neil's property, the same as the auto shop was. That meant it was legally private property, which meant we could designate it a nude beach. A significant number of the nonlocals who stayed here really did not care for a bathing suit when it came to going for a swim. And there were a couple of guests I'd spoken to in the past who'd never even heard of the concept.

I would have said something like, 'You should check out France or Germany; I've heard they're a lot more chill about nudity.' But then I'd be the world's worst hotel manager, encouraging them to vacation somewhere else.

"If you need anything at all, feel free to speak to us at the front desk," I said, finishing up my spiel as I motioned to Josh, then motioning toward the other end of the lobby, "or visit Nancy at the sundry shop from open from 8 a.m. to 5 p.m."

"Thank you so much, Manager," said Raidne, giving me a smile. They each went off with two room keys in their hands.

That's how it went for the rest of the day, with occasional questions as they arrived. One woman asked if the swimming hole had a selection of fish to choose from, which species there were, but I figured that was more of a question of, 'Should we bring snacks, or will there be some there?' They could go to the diner for meals and Andrea would leave anything uncooked for them if they asked. And whether they wanted something baked, fried, grilled, broiled, steamed, smoked, poached, or something even fancier, they could rest assured that she could do it and it would be delicious.

Another guest asked if she could fill her tub with sea water. I'd been asked this question before, and the answer was yes. "As long as nothing goes down the drain that might clog the pipes," I added. Fyfe had told me that if they ran salt water continuously, we'd likely need to overhaul the plumbing system, but occasional bath bombs, Epsom salt, or even seawater was fine.

Nobody asked about the hours at which they might play their instruments, so I assumed nobody was worried about losing sleep from it. Likely the sound of the music was soothing, like background noise. Even if there were several of them and it was loud, I'd expect it to be like someone who went to sleep to the noise of a city; sometimes you end up unable to fall asleep without it.

I also continued to get the occasional inquiring phone call. We weren't in a sprawling metropolis, but people did call to ask about rooms. "Unfortunately, we're fully booked through Saturday," I told the woman.

"All week?" she asked in surprise. "Not one room?"

"There's a group that reserved the rooms a few months in advance for the week," I told her. "So, on Sunday, we'll be back to our average availability. Would you like a referral to somewhere nearby?"

"Ah…no, thanks, I'll just check my phone."

It wasn't long before the faint scent of freshly cooked fish started wafting out of the diner, drawing guests in as they arrived, even before they'd visited their rooms, if only for an appetizer. Once dinnertime rolled around, everyone had arrived and most of them were in the diner chatting and feasting on all manner of seafood.

One of the locals who came in for dinner asked if we were having a special, and I guess he was looking for discounts or something, because he looked disappointed when I explained it was just a crowd of seafood enthusiasts. But my guess was that when it came time for him to order, he joined in anyway.

I took my dinner break during the rush, to be able to mingle with the small crowd, and they appeared to be enjoying themselves. A variety of dishes had been ordered, and I spotted some usual suspects, but also octopus and sea urchin, as well as a few things that had been chopped and cooked beyond recognition.

When Jodie walked over to take my order, I grinned and said, "Just ask Andrea to feed me." She returned the smile and nodded once.

I don't know what kind of fish it was, but it was awesome.

Toward the end of my shift, a handful of the women had settled in the lobby, chatting, and eventually wandered off. I'd assumed they'd headed to their rooms, but they came back with their instruments, three with flutes and four with lyres, and started to play.

"Holy crap," Delilah whispered, standing next to me as we gazed over at the live performance. "Step aside, New York Philharmonic."

"Yeah, this is cool," I said quietly, smiling. Isadora had been talented on her own, but seven of them playing together was incredible.

Working at this hotel did, on occasion, have its perks.

After a good night's sleep, I smiled when I consciously realized that I'd been woken by my alarm, meaning I'd slept through the night. Occasionally we had guests that were a little demanding, and there were times I'd gotten calls in the middle of the night that were urgent, but not because something was wrong. Having not been woken on the first night was a good sign. It wasn't as if they did it maliciously or rudely, that tilted too far in the direction of abusing hospitality, but some who stayed at the hotel were high maintenance.

There were six guests in the diner having breakfast when I did my walk-through, all at separate tables. When I checked in with Andrea, asking how the seafood extravaganza was going, she said extremely well. The first night of orders hadn't been any more than they could handle, which was good, since that was likely the highest the bar would be. Whenever guests arrived for a convention (as long as they hadn't trudged in after an exhausting road trip), they were typically excited and ordered a 'We're on vacation!' great meal.

"Everything else okay?" I asked, picking up on some strangeness in Andrea's demeanor.

The chef shrugged. "Yeah. The guests seem…cool. I saw all the instruments." She paused, pursing her lips. "Do you know much about them?"

"Only what I told you," I replied. "Something concerning you?"

Andrea made a grimacing, dismissive face. "You just never know what to expect. That's how it goes with this hotel."

I nodded. "Yeah. Though weirdly, the most horrible thing we've dealt with in a while was locals robbing us. Compared to that, I'll take teleporting frogs and losing sunglasses through portals any day."

Standing up straighter, anger flashing across her face, she said, "You know, that's absolutely true. Coming into my diner, scaring the shit out of my customers. Wish I could've punched them in the face a few times."

"They did flip their car and need to go to the hospital."

"I could wait until after they get out of the hospital. I'm patient."

I smirked at her, and she gave me a smile that let me know she wasn't kidding.

Walking back out through the diner, I wondered how solitary the women were day to day, and how often they had get-togethers. My guess was that after they spent some time together doing things they had in common, like hiking to the swimming hole or playing music, they'd start to get to know each other more.

Speaking of the swimming hole, there was a startling moment a couple hours later when I was at the front desk with Josh. When movement caught my attention, I glanced up to the guest that was walking by, I did a double take. "Uh-Uh, hold on!" I managed, flailing out of my chair and quickly getting out from behind the desk.

"Oh, boy," I heard Josh state, and I pictured him immediately averting his gaze.

"Leucosia, was it?" Remembering names did come in handy, but any I hadn't heard before could really challenge me.

"Yes," she said, smiling that I'd got her name right.

"I'm so sorry, but could I speak with you back in your room for a moment?" I said quickly.

Her smile dimmed but she nodded. "Sure." She turned to go back, unhurried, just as a mother and son left the diner.

"Oh!" exclaimed the woman in shock.

The boy, who'd been staring down at his phone, looked up and followed his mother's gaze. His eyes bulged in surprise, and there was a moment where everyone was still, including Leucosia, who'd caught on that something was wrong. Then the boy started to slowly lift his phone up.

I snapped up a finger, jabbing it pointedly at him, and said, "Don't you dare, or I will break it in half," as I stepped in front of Leucosia.

He grimaced and did so, sliding it into his pocket. "You're gonna break an iPhone in half?" he snarked.

"We've got knives in the kitchen that can cut through bone," I growled.

"And when she's done that, I will stick it in a blender for good measure," his mother told him, her eyes wide. "Don't you *ever* do that without someone's permission, or you will never have a phone again, do you hear me?"

"Okay, alright," he groaned as she pulled him toward the front doors.

Turning and motioning to her as I encouraged her to start walking, Leucosia and I headed back down the hallway. "Is it because I'm naked?" she asked.

"Yes," I said with a tight smile. "I should have been clearer about things here, I guess. The swimming hole is in a remote area in the forest, which makes it okay for it to be a nudist location, but you have to wear clothes here. You can disrobe when you get there."

"I see. My mistake," she said, looking mildly chagrined. "What was that about the boy and his phone?"

I cleared my throat as we reached the stairwell. "He was going to photograph you."

Leucosia's eyes narrowed dangerously. "What? Why would he do that?"

Hesitating for a moment to find the right words, I finally said, "You are a naked woman." She blinked, averting her gaze thoughtfully, considering what to make of that. "Rest assured that photos of nonlocal guests, whether they're clothed or not, cannot leave the premises."

Pausing for a moment, she muttered, "All right." Then she turned and headed back up the stairs, looking perturbed. I didn't blame her.

As I walked back behind the desk, I heard Josh speaking into the phone, saying, "Yes, I figured some of you might know, but I'm double checking now. Thank you so much." He nodded to himself and hung up before picking the phone back up and pressing the number for another room.

I watched the rookie proudly as I sat back down in my chair. "Hi, this is Josh at the front desk. We just had a misunderstanding in the lobby, and I wanted to make sure all guests know that you're permitted to be nude at the swimming hole on our property, but it is legally required for you to be clothed on your way there…"

Chapter 6

Having a hotel full of guests who all had similar preferences and requests had a way of streamlining things. When it turned out many of them simply kept their tubs full instead of emptying and refilling them, Fyfe only needed to double-check with one person to ensure they knew he would only clean them if they were empty. Also, when another woman caught a fish and wondered if Andrea would cook it for her, word quickly spread that the chef was happy to do so.

Not all of them were outgoing and social, though. One young woman in particular, Teles, introduced herself to me the next morning and asked if she could play her lyre by herself in the lobby. I guessed that she'd seen others sharing their music together and wasn't sure if solo playing would look egotistical. I assured her that anyone could play wherever they wanted, as long as it didn't disturb others.

Teles made herself comfortable on the center cushion of the sofa, folding her legs under her. She didn't start to play right away though. Instead, she placed her instrument aside and leaned back into the cushion behind her, splaying her arms out to her sides and letting out a long, calming breath.

"Do all of them have instruments, you think?" Josh asked.

I thought for a moment. "Maybe. Or maybe only half of them, the same way they're divided up by floor?"

Josh nodded slowly.

Thinking back, Isadora had been so talented just on her own, at a professional level, as I'm sure all of them were. And she'd clearly taken her music very seriously, by the reaction to another guest wanting to drop a mere dollar in a cup as a tip. To have several of them get together and harmonize, play a song that they all knew and loved? It really had been beautiful.

My attention went back to Teles though, as I heard her start to pluck the strings of the lyre. Her eyes were still closed, and she started gently and slowly, though the pace picked up a few moments into the song. I smiled as warmth bloomed in my chest. The pianist we had come in could play magnificently, but he only came in a couple days a month. Having a whole week of live music was wonderful.

Walking toward her before I'd even decided to do so, I slowly sat down in a loveseat, easing into the cushions. If only all our guests were like this, my job would be so much more laid-back. Sure, there were occasionally miscommunications and confusions with the peculiar guests, but they were generally polite and did things like hang out and play music. It's not like I wanted to work at a health resort and listen to yoga music all day, but having interludes of someone sharing their musical talent was fantastic.

Until she was punched in the jaw.

Jerked out of my reverie with a start, I realized I'd closed my eyes and now blinked rapidly. I stared in astonishment at Andrea, whose chest was heaving with exertion, tears streaming down her face. I looked around in a daze, realizing that Josh, Nancy, the two servers, two cooks, and three customers who had been in the diner were also standing around us.

Some of them started muttering amongst themselves as I pushed myself to my feet. "What in the hell?" I managed, looking from Andrea to the musician, who was rubbing her jaw and staring at my coworker in shock.

"That's my question too," Andrea spat, glaring at the woman. "What the fuck do you think you're doing?"

"Why-Why did you strike me?" she whimpered.

"Look around!" she shouted. "Why do you think?"

The woman's wide eyes flicked to each of us in turn. "Oh…Oh no…"

"Crap, I've got something on the stove," one of the cooks said suddenly, turning and rapidly heading back to the kitchen.

"Ah geez," Nancy said, a tone of exhaustion in her voice. She rubbed her hands up and down her face before turning and walking back to the sundry shop.

Andrea's jaw was tight and her fists were clenched, so I moved in between her and Teles, catching my friend's gaze. When I did that, the chef wiped at her face, clearing it of the tears she'd shed. I'd learned to take in information quickly in this gig, and it didn't take a genius to realize the music had brought us all out here. But there was still obviously something I was missing from Andrea, and this had become a spectacle.

"All right, the concert's over, everyone. As you were." I vaguely gestured away from us and the others disbursed. Josh went back to the front desk, and my eyes narrowed. We were nearby, but still, the front desk shouldn't have been left unattended when neither of us were busy. We didn't *choose* to walk over.

"Andrea, what just happened?" I asked her, my voice hushed.

"She broke hospitality," Andrea growled.

At that, the woman hissed in a breath through her teeth, sounding upset and alarmed at the accusation.

"How?" I asked softly.

"Her instrument dragged every human within range over to listen," Andrea said. Her expression concerned me, since it looked like she was on the verge of more furious tears but determined not to shed them. "It took me a minute, but I managed to jolt my mind out of it long enough to get her to stop. I just want to find out if it was an accident, or if she knew and didn't care."

"I see." Looking back at our guest, I met her gaze. "Teles, I'm assuming you were attempting to attract one of the guests, but were you aware of how your music affects humans?"

Teles looked regretful. "It didn't occur to me." She grimaced and shook her head, looking at me and then to Andrea. "I'm terribly sorry. It's been decades since I've played around others, but there's no excuse for my lapse in judgment. My mind has been fixated on my own kind since I arrived, and unconcerned with others present. I was…I was shy and nervous, so I leaned on my music to reach out to the others, since it's easier."

"Well, Andrea didn't have many other options other than to hit you," I said slowly. "It seems that it was a struggle for her just to keep her wits about herself." Teles stared at her hands and nodded. After a thoughtful pause, I looked to Andrea. "What happened affected all of us, but clearly it legitimately hurt you," I said. Her face twitched in discontent. "Do you want her expelled from this event? Or banned?"

Andrea folded her arms tightly, averting her gaze, and Teles didn't say a word. She just kept quiet, hunched over, her hands clasped in her lap, her lyre on the cushion beside her. "No," Andrea finally whispered. "But I do not want this happening again."

"Absolutely," I said with a nod. "Teles, please go door to door and explain that music to attract a mate is forbidden while at the crossroads, because of the presence of humans. If anyone is not in their room, check the diner, and let us know if there was anyone you couldn't find. I'll jot down a message and leave it taped to their door."

"Of course," the woman said quietly, pushing herself to her feet. "My deepest apologies again, Manager. And to you as well, chef Andrea." At that, Andrea swiftly marched off to the kitchen without another word. Teles looked lost in her thoughts as she turned and walked toward the hall.

I heard her knock on the first door just as I stepped up to the front of the reception desk. "We're okay," I said.

"Right, so…that was disturbing," Josh said tiredly. "Can I make a guess out loud as to who our guests are?"

"Sirens?" I said. "Yeah. Them, I've heard of. Look, I need to speak to Andrea. I'll be back in a few minutes." Josh nodded and I headed to the diner. The guests had taken their seats and resumed eating, and I saw one server talking to one of them and another at the register getting a receipt for a table.

Walking to the kitchen, I spoke up, "Coming in!" and pushed in the door on the right. Letting it swing shut behind me, I saw the cooks back at their stations, but no sign of Andrea.

"She's in the break room," said Patrick, one of our two cooks, looking like he'd been expecting me.

Letting out a long breath, I nodded once and went to the back of the kitchen to the door on the left, going through the open doorway. Andrea was sitting with a bottle of bourbon open on the table in front of her. She took a drink directly from the bottle as I walked in and sat down but didn't say anything.

I remained silent. She knew why I was here. If she'd told me she didn't want to talk about it, I would've left it alone, and instead just gotten myself a glass to have a drink with her. Whatever it was, obviously it was painful, and I didn't want to leave her to stew in her feelings alone. But before long, she started talking.

"Almost two decades ago, I was married with two kids in St. Louis," she said. Andrea spoke to the bottle on the table rather than me. "Worked as a cook at a real nice place. Dinner place, open half the week, late hours. I was absolute fire in that kitchen. Then they hired Mike. Mike Braxton." She slowly turned the bottle on the table, so the label was facing her. "The first week, he got to know me. The second week, we were flirting. The third week, we were out back, fucking against the wall next to the dumpster."

Andrea took another drink and let out a shaky breath. "It was like my brain had been split in two. A level of cognitive dissonance I didn't think I was capable of. I didn't know what was going on, why I was doing that to Cameron. My husband," she clarified, blinking. "I didn't know where my feelings for Mike exploded from. I fucking loved my husband. He was my soul mate.

"One night after work, I went to a bar and got nice and drunk. Sat there for a while before I took a taxi home. Kids were already in bed, and I just *jumped* Cameron. We had the most amazing night, and he didn't know what the occasion was, but he was all in. I woke up the next morning, he'd already gone to work, and I was in the bathroom in a flash, vomiting up everything short of my stomach lining. Because I loved him so damn much, and when I was with him it's like my life was still like it used to be, but the feelings for Mike were still layered on top. I just felt disgusting."

Shaking her head, Andrea rubbed at her face. "I went into work that evening and told Mike I wanted to stop things with him. Told him I loved Cameron. By the end of the conversation, we were in the closet making out." She gnashed her teeth, her face cold and furious. "Felt like I was trapped in some hell dimension. So, I decided not to mess around, to just get straight to the point and fight off whatever was going on by killing my libido as quickly and effectively as possible. Can't cheat if I can't feel, right? I went to a friend of a friend, who knew someone that sold heroin. Stocked up. I lied to Cameron about my hours being extended, so I could do it before work."

A long silence stretched before she spoke again. "You believe that? I started doing heroin to try to save my marriage."

"I believe it," I said quietly. I considered telling her she didn't have to explain everything, not if it hurt, but she was one of my best friends. If she wanted to get this out, there wasn't anything I would do to stop her.

"I mean, I couldn't quit my job, 'cause Mike made it clear he was in love with me, and that he'd follow me anywhere. I had nightmares of him showing up at my house, messing with Cameron or the boys. So, yeah. I slowly started to build up this…wall in my head. Fighting back against him."

Andrea snorted and took a long drink from the bourbon. "Then Cameron found out about the heroin. Because of course he did, we were married. I was too mortified to tell him the truth, and it sounded so nuts, that I just let it all fall apart instead and pretended I'd started from stress. I told my boss, and they fired me, and I went into rehab. That…sucked. And things between me and Cameron were never the same. I realized he knew I'd been having an affair; he'd gone with the strategy of ignoring it and hoping it would go away. But the drugs were a step too far." She held up a finger, a motion to note an important point. "But it gets better."

"After I got out, I had enough old friends and talent that I got another job as a cook. My second day there, Mike was waiting for me outside when I left." My eyes widened. "He was livid, dragged me into an alley, had me shoved up against a wall, shouting at me, asking how I could do that to him. How I could reject him and hurt him like that. I managed to get one of my knives from my bag and stabbed him. But guess what happens when you stab something that isn't human?"

Tears burned behind my nose at the expression on my friend's face.

"Nothing, that's what. Well, he was bleeding," she corrected. "Then he hit me with this…*wave* of overwhelming love. How much I loved him in that moment made me feel like I'd slit my husband's throat. Worse, even. But something in my head managed to separate my feelings from it, enough for me to keep control. So, I stabbed him again. Twice. He finally let go of me and I ran back to the restaurant. They called the cops. I told them it was someone I used to get high with and they took photos of the bruises, filed a report, and put a warrant out for his arrest."

At that point, Andrea smiled and looked at me. It was crooked and strained, but she did. "That's when I decided, fuck logic, I know what this man's been doing to me. What this *thing* is doing to me. So, I took a day off work to 'recover from the attack' and went to the city's herbal, crystal shops. You know the ones. Spent a morning going from one to another, like down a rabbit hole. After a trail of referrals toward someone who really knew their shit, I met a woman named Caitlin. Her reaction when I told her what happened to me… I knew she understood.

"She had me wait in the back room for an hour, and a friend of hers dropped by with this anklet. Didn't look like something out of a horror movie; it was just something stitched with beads. Could've been made by a kid at summer camp. But he told me it'd make sure Mike couldn't use his compulsion on me. That's what he called it. Compulsion. I wore it for like two weeks, but then they found Mike with his head cut off in a dumpster."

I blinked rapidly. "Wait, what?"

"Yeah," she sighed. Taking another long drink from the bottle, she put it down with a *clunk*. "Cameron was the one who found out, he saw it on the news. He told me when I got back from work and...I could tell he was disturbed about how relieved I looked." She shook her head. "I still have the anklet, up in my apartment. I'm gonna find out if it'd work here too. Or if it's out of juice after all this time or something.

"But things had gone wrong with Cameron; I'd screwed it all up. Long story short, six months later, we got divorced. He got full custody of the boys and I just had visitation. I buried myself in my work, I had long hours at the restaurant, and I barely saw them. And then one Sunday night after my shift, I just started driving and driving..."

When she paused for a moment, I finished with, "And you ended up here."

Andrea smirked. "Yeah. Just felt right. It felt safe. I stayed the night, and had breakfast the next morning. Nancy asked me about the anklet. When I brushed it off, she...*really* asked."

"Nancy could tell what it was?" I asked in surprise.

"That was my reaction. We got to talking, she introduced me to Mr. Lucero, and he said the place could use a chef of my caliber. That's what he said. Not a cook; he called me a chef."

I didn't say anything, but I'd seen enough television that I knew the difference. Swallowing hard, I hesitated. "What are their names?"

Andrea took a breath. "Nathan and Carl. They're doing great," she whispered, her eyes back on the bottle. "I've always sent them holiday cards and birthday money. And after a while, I told Cameron college would be on me, no student loans. Tips took care of that. What pisses me off in hindsight, though, is that I could've saved myself a lot of trouble if I'd found Caitlin first instead of heroin. Because she's the one that passed on word of what was going on, and a few degrees of separation from her is the person who took Mike's head off."

I stared at her for a long moment, my mind spinning. "Someone figured out what he was."

"Incubus," Andrea said, meeting my gaze. "Mr. Lucero told me he'd heard about Mike being taken out; that's how rare it is for one of them to go psycho like Mike did. Lucero asked around for info for me, and then explained to me that Caitlin told someone in the know, who told someone that did the work, who told someone in charge. Whenever something like this happens, if one of them starts hurting humans, there are no second chances." She shrugged. "Which is nice to know."

As she took another drink from her bottle, I clasped my hands in my lap tightly. "That...fucking sucks," I told her. "I am so sorry that happened to you."

She nodded. "Thanks."

"Talk to Nancy, ask her if the anklet is still good," I said, "or if you need something else. Whatever it is, I don't want you having to work here with this crowd without it."

Andrea gave me a small smile. "That's the plan."

"You want the rest of the night off?"

She paused and then shook her head, picking up the top for the bottle in front of her and twisting it back on. "I think...I'm gonna make some chili. Get a big old chuck roast and break out the cleaver. Have some nice, violent kitchen therapy."

I raised an eyebrow. "You gonna share?"

Andrea smirked. "Come by when my shift's over. But I'm making the real stuff, good enough to make my fingers feel spicy, so bring a gallon of milk if you need it."

"I'm from Texas," I replied. "I wouldn't have it any other way."

Chapter 7

"You know one of the best, easiest ways to bother a medium until they do what you want? Follow them into the bathroom."

"No," I stated.

"Yes," Josh said with a nod. "Didn't happen often. But I literally had to accuse them of being a pedophile before they decided to try other strategies."

Josh was leaning back in his chair at the reception desk, a long-suffering look on his face, recounting the stories that made him glad to work in a place that didn't allow ghosts. We kept our voices quiet, as he wasn't keen on the idea of broadcasting his ability to everyone. Not even all the other employees knew.

It had taken two years for Josh to tell his parents that he saw dead people, when at the age of eight he was finally faced with the fact that it wasn't going away, and having long ago figured out that they weren't hallucinations. Once his parents realized what he was dealing with and how they could help, they insisted on accompanying him when he needed to speak to someone or do something on a spirit's behalf. There was no way they'd let their kid just take a bus around the city, following some ghost's directions. Once he was eighteen, he started doing things on his own, having learned by then how to navigate those conversations.

"There was one lady who sang opera," Josh said, his eyes widening. "Ah, geez, that was an experience. She didn't even do it to aggravate me. She just loved to sing to people, and I was the only audience member she could find."

"Was she at least good?" I asked with a smirk.

He chuckled. "Yeah, she was good. That could've been a lot worse, I guess. Then there was this old guy, Jeff, who kept going on about how his son was spending his inheritance on all the wrong stuff. His son was in his forties, by the way," he said pointedly. "Complained about other stuff too, but I'll spare you the details. When we talked to his son, the guy was in total disbelief, and started apologizing profusely. Clearly his father had been just as infuriating when he'd been alive. The whole time his son was growing up and until the day he died, Jeff's opinion had to be heard, and if his advice wasn't taken, a lecture would always follow."

"That is seriously going the extra mile," I grimaced. "Staying around after you die to keep lecturing your fully grown kids. Wow."

Josh nodded. "Yup. I'm sure they aren't the majority. Most spirits don't struggle with any of that stuff or else we'd be overrun."

I opened my mouth to reply but stopped when I noticed the front doors opening and a woman rushed in, up to the front desk. My memory did a brief rewind, realizing that she'd walked out a moment earlier.

"There-There's something-" She leaned on the counter, wide-eyed and alarmed. "It- There was something around the corner of-of the building. It's *huge*."

I straightened, concerned. "What did it look like?"

She appeared reluctant, but eventually said, "A…spider. But it was… It must've been five feet tall." Her face twitched fearfully. "Is there some crazy person with a costume trying to scare people? Could I have- Am I hallucinating?"

"How about I walk you to your car?" I said with a gentle smile, turning and walking out from behind the desk. The woman looked skeptical but followed me outside, staring toward the east end of the building warily.

Once she'd sped out of the parking lot, I shook my head and walked down to the end of the building and around the corner. I looked around and up, but there was nothing there. I did see blood on the ground, though, which shifted gears in my brain. Starting to walk back toward the entrance, I took out my walkie, turning the knob to channel two. "Marjorie for Fyfe."

"Go for Fyfe."

"I think a guest spotted Iktómi," I told him. "I would let her be, but I found some blood on the ground, around the corner of the east side of the building. I'll check on her and call you back in a few minutes. Could you clean up the blood? Over."

"Copy that, lass. Hope she's alright. Fyfe out."

Going back into the lobby and behind the desk, I pulled out the med kit. "I'll explain when I get back," I told Josh, who looked inquisitive. "Might have a guest who needs help."

"Sure thing," he replied.

Walking to the other side of the lobby, I took the stairs up to the roof entrance, pushing open the heavy door. The roof was where employees hung out on breaks sometimes, a wide-open sprawl of concrete. We had a wooden picnic table and a few ashtrays, but no trash bin, since we didn't want to encourage people to leave anything up there that would attract bugs. Everyone had to clean up after themselves and bring trash back inside.

"Iktómi?" I asked worriedly.

Sitting on the ground, leaning against the four-foot wall that surrounded the roof, the woman was holding one arm tightly across her chest with the other. I went over to her, putting down the med kit and crouching. She looked pale, and with some nonlocals I would be subtle and skirt around the issue, but she was a repeat guest, and I was fond of her. "Are you okay?" I asked directly.

"Oh, I'll be fine, Manager," she said with an appreciative smile. "I just came to the hotel to take a break from some difficulties. Your concern is appreciated."

Questions about what had happened would've been nosey, so I dodged the topic. "Can I help?"

Iktómi's face softened. I guessed that she would've been fine on her own, for all I knew she had super-healing powers, but I felt compelled to offer assistance on at least a basic level for a generously bleeding injury. She was probably thinking about how fussy humans were over the smallest things. "Gauze to wrap the wound would be useful," she finally said.

Taking out a pair of blue medical gloves and pulling them on, I took out the roll of large gauze and pulled out a stretch of it. Removing her left arm, Iktómi revealed a deep gash that almost went the length of her right arm. I hissed in a breath through my teeth. "Jesus," I whispered.

"No, wasn't him. Someone else."

I bit my lower lip, smothering a smirk, as I carefully placed the end of the gauze near her wrist and started to wrap it. It seemed to have almost completely clotted already. I slowly enclosed the arm in the gauze, trying to make it just tight enough to put a little pressure and ensure it wouldn't start bleeding again. Once I finished and used the scissors to cut it, I just tucked it into a fold so it would be easy to remove.

"There we go," I murmured. "Painkillers?"

"No, thank you."

I took off the gloves, which turned them inside-out, and shoved them into my pocket for disposal later. Then I closed up the med kit. "Are you staying the night? I could get you something from the kitchen."

"I planned to, yes," Iktómi said, "but I'll just come down for dinner later. I'd like to rest first."

I took hold of the med kit's handle and stood up, giving her a small smile. "Sleep well."

"Thank you."

Iktómi occasionally checked into the hotel, but usually she just came here for the food. That's probably not surprising to you at this point; many guests do. But she was the only guest I knew of that preferred to sleep up on the roof. It wasn't that she had a preference for concrete; she slept in a hammock of her own making, slung across one corner of the wall.

That fact is on a list of things that I tell new employees when they first start working here. It's important because while I call it a hammock, it's really more of a cocoon.

As I walked down the stairs, I got back on the walkie, letting Fyfe know that everything was cool and that Iktómi was staying the night. When I got back to the desk, it was just in time to see a man walk in through the front doors. He was wearing an off the rack suit, and looked tired, which was worrying since it was only about eleven in the morning. I met his gaze in greeting as I walked behind the desk.

"Hi, I really need a room," he told me.

"Unfortunately, we have no vacancies at the moment," I replied. Tact kept me from pointing out that the sign outside was lit up with that very information. Not wanting to assume he had a smartphone to find the info he needed, I gave my standard reply. "The nearest decent selection of hotels is in St. Robert. I'm not sure what direction you were headed, though, if that might be back the way you came."

He let out a ragged breath in exasperation. "I wanted to stay *here*," he said. "Expedia said there were rooms. I've had the worst night, and I just want a bed. How are *all* your rooms booked? It's a Monday."

"We have a convention going on through the whole week," I explained. "Sometimes the travel websites get it wrong, though it likely wouldn't have let you reserve a room if you'd tried, and so we always encourage our guests to check our own website."

"This isn't my fault, I'm not an idiot," he snapped, raising his voice. "It said you had rooms available."

"I understand that, sir," I said with faux patience.

"Can you double check? Maybe someone checked out and you weren't told?"

Movement caught my attention as I saw one of the guests slow to a stop a few yards away at the commotion, looking like she'd been going toward the diner. She had told me her name at check-in, but I couldn't recall it. Something starting with a P. "Sir, I'm the Manager. I would know if we had a room available."

"You won't even bother to check the damn computer?" he asked. "What if my phone was right?"

"Excuse me," spoke the woman, walking over. "Why are you yelling?"

He glared at her, giving her a once-over, and purposefully lowered his voice before saying, "I'm not yelling. I just want a room."

"We booked the hotel for the week," she said simply. "There are no rooms."

The man glanced at the seating area in the lobby, where four women were comfortably settled, chatting. "What is this, some kind of freaky Kumbaya cult or something?" Presumably he was referring to the tunics they were wearing, and my eyes narrowed in annoyance.

"Kumbaya is a spiritual song presumed to have originated among African Americans," the guest told him, looking puzzled. "I'm from Korea."

He stared at her with wide eyes, and I wasn't sure how he was going to take that. "What, are you calling me racist?" he finally snapped.

She looked even more confused at that. "Why would that be racist?"

"Oh, I get it, it's a dyke convention," he said accusingly. I followed his gaze, looking at two women who were cozying up together on the sofa, clasping hands, as one of the others picked up their lyre. "Do you really need to have those here, and take over entire hotels?"

The woman's expression shifted, becoming stern and irritated. "If you're curious, I don't believe you were being racist, but *that* was homophobic," she said. "It's surreal to me how enough time can destroy anything. The full comprehension of love in Ancient Greek society was three thousand years ago, and look at you now."

The man's face started to turn red. "Go to Hell," he growled.

"When people say that, which Hell do they mean?" she asked, turning to me. "I've wanted clarification on that for some time."

That prompted me to smile, amused. "The Christian one, where you're set on fire for eternity."

"Ah. What an image," she said, scrunching her nose. She gave the man an annoyed look before walking off toward the diner and he glared after her before turning back to me.

"You're telling me all the rooms are taken up by one woman each, when they're literally here to sleep with each other?" he said, scowling at me.

"They're having a dating event. This isn't a brothel," I stated. "Do you speak French, by any chance? Or Swahili?"

"What?"

"If you're having a hard time understanding my English, I thought maybe Josh could explain to you that we have no empty rooms in another language," I said, gesturing to my coworker.

He scowled at me furiously. "Are you being aggravating on purpose? When did hotels start hiring teenage girls as managers anyway?"

I glared at him. He was the one being purposefully aggravating. I'd had friends in college who were peeved at how young they look, but I knew I looked twenty-four. The next few years of my life would be spent figuring out whether

I wanted to keep growing or not, but he was making me think I'd be happier if I waited until I was at least forty to stop aging normally.

"Hey," Josh said, standing up. "I think it's time for you to go." It seemed he'd reached his limit with this guy too. The women in the lobby had started staring as well, which was frustrating. I dealt with assholes all the time, but they shouldn't have had to.

"Right. Someone still in high school telling me what's what, that'll clear things up," he said with a wave of his hand at Josh.

"Look, I don't know what your issue is with people doing their job while committing the awful crime of still being young, but it *is* time for you to go," I told him tersely. "See that right there?" I pointed at the wood-carved sign describing the guide for being a hospitable guest in the hotel, declaring that the guests agreed to them, and that we had a right to eject anyone who violated them. "We are consistently hospitable to people who visit us, but it is a social contract between us and them. You don't get to act however you want in the face of it."

"Is that right?" He jabbed a finger at the computer. "I'm not leaving until you check if there's a room available! Either do that, or get your boss on the phone so I can tell him how shitty you are to your guests."

That didn't so much push my buttons as punch them repeatedly. "My boss has better things to do than deal with every entitled prick who comes in here," I finally snapped at him. "And you are *not* a guest. You are someone who walked in here demanding something I cannot give you."

"Entitled prick?" he barked. "Who do you think you are, you bitch?"

"Hey!" Josh shouted at him.

I gritted my teeth, taking a slow breath to push back the infuriating burn of tears I felt threatening me from behind my nose. "There aren't any rooms available. And I'm not allowed to let guests sleep on the couch. And even if you wanted to sleep on the roof, I wouldn't let you. Get out of my hotel!"

"*Your* hotel?" he shouted, a hint of mockery in his tone. "And you say I'm entitled. Give a kid a name tag and they think they rule the world. Newsflash: you literally sit here at a desk all day and occasionally poke at the computer. How about you call the man who actually owns this place? And I can let him know how horribly you treat people that walk in here, so he can throw you out on your ass and find someone who *can* do this job?"

A heavy beat passed where the silence between us felt crushing, and then the wall I'd built cracked and broke as I choked out a single sob, tears spilling from my eyes.

"Seriously?" he groaned. I wiped them away and held my breath to keep from letting it happen again. "I am so done with you."

"My thoughts exactly."

I blinked and looked to my right, where the guest from a few minutes earlier was now standing. Then a moment later, the man stumbled backwards, like gravity was shifting under his feet, his hands going to his head, and he collapsed to the ground.

The shock of it startled me out of my despair and I exhaled sharply, gawking. No one moved for a few seconds.

"Is he dead?" Josh asked. From his tone, it didn't seem as if that possibility bothered him.

"Oh. No," the woman said casually. "I assumed that would be a nuisance."

"Right… Yeah it…would be a nuisance."

The man made a small sound, twitching, before he slowly brought a hand to his forehead. His eyes were still closed, and he lowered his other hand flat against the floor, as if steadying himself against it would keep him from falling off.

"Manager," the woman said softly, drawing my gaze. I swallowed, wiping away the remnants of tears. "I hope I did not overstep on your authority with my actions. I felt he was violating hospitality and transgressing so severely that it needed to be stopped."

On my authority… "Not at all," I whispered. "Thank you. Apologies, but I forgot your name."

At that, she smiled broadly and with a hint of pride. "Parthenope," she said. Then she turned to walk back to the diner.

Chapter 8

No sooner had Parthenope departed, heading to the diner for either a late breakfast or early lunch, then two of the women who'd been sitting on the couch walked over. They stood one on either side of the man splayed out on the floor, hands on their hips as they stared down at him. His eyelids started to flutter, then managed to open, and he looked up at them with a befuddled expression. "Wha' 'appened?" he grunted.

"You have some sort of blood pressure problem, dude?" Josh asked, leaning forward with his forearms on the counter. "You dropped like a sack of bricks. There's a GP in the office complex. Maybe get yourself checked out."

The man unsteadily managed to sit up, and after a few beats, slowly lifted himself to his feet with the help of the two guests. "We'll help you out to your car," said one of them, her voice sweet as sugar.

"Alright," he muttered.

He was escorted out, one woman holding each arm to keep him stable on wobbly feet, and the doors shut behind them.

"You okay?"

I pursed my lip and blinked a few times, folding my arms tightly. "Fine."

"Listen…I know you're taking things at your own pace," Josh said, his serious tone drawing my gaze, "but I think you need to talk to someone."

"What, about the fact that I have to deal with assholes at my job?"

He looked at me reproachfully. "I've seen you deal with people like him dozens of times. That's not what that was." I slid my gaze down to my feet. "I don't have to have a PhD to know that my friend is struggling. And I know you wanted to just take things one day at a time, manage it on your own, but this is too big. Not only that, you shouldn't *have to* deal with it alone."

Chuckling, I shook my head. "What, so I should call someone from the giant selection of therapists that work at this intersection? Or should I make a Zoom appointment? I'm sure the crossroads would be happy to let me talk to a random human somewhere about how I'm having a hard time adjusting to being dead."

"No, I'm saying that Mr. Lucero must know at least one mental health professional that you'd be allowed to talk to, either here or on Zoom."

Blinking, I narrowed my eyes thoughtfully. It hadn't even occurred to me to go to my boss on that, but it wasn't a bad idea. The truth was, I was floundering. Even if I hadn't died, I probably would've seen a therapist eventually for the issues that had built up through my childhood as I'd clashed with my parents.

But now things were exponentially worse. I was suffering, and I'd known I was suffering, but it hadn't felt like there was any other option but to keep doing what I'd been doing. I was a train, on a set of tracks that only led one direction, and I could slow down and speed up, but that was about it. Also, I had been fine for two years, I loved it here, and I'd figured once I came to terms with what had happened, my mind would acclimatize to the new situation. It seemed, however, that things wouldn't be that easy.

"I didn't think about asking him," I said quietly, meeting Josh's gaze. "It's a good idea. Thanks." He gave me a small smile.

Sitting back down in my chair and leaning back with a heavy sigh, I wondered how a therapist would tackle my problems. Whether the nonhuman world also had banal commercials, advertising mental health services to the deceased with an empathetic, kind woman doing a voiceover.

'Just because you're dead, doesn't mean your feelings are. For those still on Earth but cut off from everyone and everything you knew, there's help. Call now to set up an appointment, or to have a session over the phone if your appearance is still disturbingly bloody from your gruesome demise.'

Gratefully, the rest of the day didn't hold any more surprises. That night, after my shift ended, I emailed Mr. Lucero, asking if he could give me a referral to a mental health professional that was crossroads-approved. He messaged me back only an hour later, giving me the names of three who were currently accepting new patients, with thorough descriptions of each. The weight on my shoulders felt a little lighter, just knowing they were available.

But I still got halfway into a bottle of wine while watching reruns of The Office before bed.

Opening my eyes after waking naturally a little before 9:00 a.m., I enjoyed the peaceful feeling of waking up to my day off, remaining sprawled out in bed for a while until I started to get bored. Then I stretched, slid out of bed, and went about my morning routine.

I considered making my own breakfast, which would let me stay up in my room instead of heading down to the hotel, but as it often did, the desire for someone else to cook for me won out. Andrea almost always made my orders, declaring that the boss got nothing but the best from her kitchen. The exception was our day off, but the food from the other cooks was nothing to scoff at and my mouth was already watering.

Andrea had once noted her dedication to making sure my food was always perfect, laying it on quite thick, that she was in no way doing it to make sure she kept being my favorite employee. I'd mentioned that I don't have favorites, and she dismissively went, "Oh, right, of course," but then gave me a wink.

The diner was quite crowded, since the hotel was full and we also had the typical number of locals, all either chatting as they waited for their food or pausing their conversation to eat. We often get long-haul truckers, who are the type to try and find the best local places to stop on their routes for a meal. And since we have an auto shop and the plaza of stores across the street, quite a few of them end up finding the hotel's diner.

My order came out before too long. Blueberry pancakes, two eggs sunny-side-up, and two slices of bacon. I leaned my elbows on the table and ate slowly, appreciating every bite. Glancing around to the hotel's guests, I saw four women paired up that I'd seen together before. I wondered if they'd already felt the tug of interest, and had started having conversations that began to form bonds.

It seemed obvious to me that two days wasn't enough to figure out who you wanted to live with for the rest of your life, but this would be a great starting point. That was looking at it from a human perspective, though. I didn't know how long they lived, or whether they stayed together forever, or even if they were monogamous. It reminded me of what it would be like figuring out whether I'd want a partner in the future; there are many variables at play.

Putting aside the thought, earmarking it for therapy, I finished my breakfast and went back upstairs. Speaking of head-shrinking, I'd decided the previous night on which of the therapists Mr. Lucero had recommended with whom I wanted to make an appointment. I called and spoke to her receptionist, who let me know she had an opening the next Wednesday afternoon.

Whether out of generosity or some other unknown factors, I was told we'd have the appointment in person in an office in the complex that was kitty-corner to us in the intersection. I gave some basic information, and the woman let me know she'd email me the paperwork I needed to get done beforehand.

Then I headed into my art room. I always had a few unfinished projects, since sometimes I lost interest in a painting or suddenly had a desire to work on something else in particular. The latter was the case today. I took out a new canvas, wanting to start a fresh painting from a photo I'd printed out, with the best paints I had.

It was a photo of me and my parents, one on either side of me, at a local fairground. I'd been twelve, I think, and had a half-finished giant puff of cotton candy in my hand. The photo was taken by a passerby, our expressions happy and at ease in the way of a family who'd put everyday stresses aside to go on our favorite rides, play exorbitantly priced games, and eat too much greasy, sugary food.

I'd already decided to hang the painting in a prominent spot on a wall in my art room.

First came sketching it out with a graphite pencil. The minutes passed by like seconds as my mind focused on the outline I was prepping, glancing back and forth from the photo. Then it was eventually time to get started, and then it was just me, the brush in my hand, and the task of putting paint on the canvas. It always required just enough focus to keep my brain from wandering, but little enough to relax, letting muscle memory and instinct guide my work.

Stretching intermittently, taking water breaks, and then heating up some leftovers for lunch, I got quite far into the project. At one point, I sat on the floor in front of my easel, letting the memories flow through me. Eventually tears came to my eyes, and I let them, wiping them away as they slid down my cheeks.

Eventually it came time for dinner, and I scrubbed my hands clean, getting all the paint off at the sink in the art room, before a final wash with hand soap. As always, though, little slivers of color hid under my closely trimmed fingernails. I usually cleaned them out, but on my day off I often left it for the next morning.

Two of our day players, Jim and Katrina, were at the front desk as expected, and they gave me a wave in greeting, which I returned. All four department heads had today off, and their schedule was covered by someone else, though we could be called on for emergencies. The employees that stood in for us were people who worked elsewhere in the crossroads, mostly part-time.

Heading into the diner, I smiled curiously as I saw the larger tables occupied not only by guests who'd come for dinner, but also some playing board games. Boxes had been piled on one of the unused tables, and I saw the ones most people knew, like chess, checkers, and backgammon, and also Scrabble. But amusingly, I also saw four women deep into a game of Monopoly.

"Who's winning?" I asked with a smile, looking over the board.

"I don't know, but I'm definitely losing," sighed Ligeia. "I don't know why I let them talk me into joining in. I've only played it once before, I hated it then, and I hate it now."

"That can be a common sentiment when it comes to this game," I said.

Ligeia looked up to me. "How is it that something that was supposed to show the unsustainability of landlords became one of the most popular games on this planet?"

Chuckling, I shook my head. "People love irony, I guess."

"People are appalling," she groused.

"You wouldn't say that if you'd managed to get Park Place," said another woman in a sing-song voice. Ligeia simply raised an eyebrow, and I wandered off to find an empty table.

Of course, I'd long memorized the standard menu, adjusting the list in my head whenever Andrea made changes, so Gabriel stopped by to take my order without bothering to bring me one. Also, I could always order things off-menu. Craving carbs, I went with chicken fettuccini alfredo and garlic bread. Nearby were two women hunched over a chessboard in concentration, and I watched the game progress.

My mind wandered, though, as it is wont to do, I found myself thinking of everything I wanted to discuss with my therapist. When I got to the point where my brain was trying to tackle it on my own, I deliberately brought my thoughts back to the chess game. After I finished my dinner, I stayed to watch the remainder and see who won.

Then I found myself wandering up to the roof. The sun wasn't going to set for another hour or so, so the stars weren't out, but it was still always a pleasant place to hang out. Iktómi was still there, a white silk cocoon slung right where it always was. I hoped she was healing up well.

Curiously, there was also a guest up there, the woman who'd caused the asshole to pass out, sitting on the picnic table bench and playing her lyre. This time I remembered her name – Parthenope. At the sound of the door opening, she'd glanced over to me, but her music didn't falter. I gave her a smile and she returned it before looking back out over the stretch of trees that extended a ways south of the building. Sitting down on the bench a few feet away from her, I leaned forward, elbows on my knees, as I enjoyed the music.

Once the song came to a natural conclusion, she set the instrument aside and said, "Are you enjoying your day off, Manager?"

"Couldn't have come at a better time," I replied with a wry smile, sitting up straight.

Parthenope rolled her eyes. "Indeed. I heard that that man sat in his car for a while, gathering himself, and then went over to see the doctor. Something about worrying about his blood pressure. I do hope that poor dear is all right, Manager," she said, a facetious note in her earnest tone.

I smirked. "Yes, he must have been quite concerned. And please, call me Marjorie."

"Marjorie, then." She paused before saying, "If I may be so bold, it seemed that his words struck a nerve, even though what he's saying should have rung hollow. Your reputation as Manager is…contrary to what I saw. May I ask if you're alright?"

I gave her a small smile and nodded slowly. "That's kind of you. I've been struggling for the past few weeks. I… I found out that I'm dead," I said softly. "That I died in a car crash when I arrived, and the crossroads manifested me."

Usually I kept things to myself, especially big things like this, but I felt the sudden urge to spill out what I was feeling. Everyone who'd been told what happened was a friend of mine, and the therapist would be discussing it in a mental health capacity. I just wanted to talk to someone who knew things like this could happen but had no real stake in it. Just an objective viewpoint.

Parthenope's expression turned despairing. "I had no idea. If the crossroads manifested you, though, then that means…"

I nodded. "I can't leave. It's not a huge deal, because everything I need is here, but it's still been a lot to absorb."

"Absolutely." She worried at her lower lip. "Is that why he was able to hurt you? Because you're already feeling sad?"

Considering the question for a long moment, I shook my head. What I was going through was a giant contributing factor, of course, but it wasn't quite that simple.

"It was what he was saying," I admitted. "That I was some little girl laboring under the delusion that I have an important job. Saying my job isn't hard, that I'm replaceable. This job is half of my life. If Mr. Lucero decides that there's someone better suited that he wants to hire in a year, or five years, or ten, I could still work here, but I'd probably be an assistant manager. And I don't have a real life anymore, so I've got no room to grow."

Parthenope stared at me, her face looking somewhere between shocked and bewildered. "Someone better suited?" she echoed. "Marjorie, that's not what your job is. It's not like one you had while you were in the world of most who live on this plane. To be called to be the Manager of a place like this, there is no *replacement*. The crossroads doesn't make mistakes like that, and it doesn't entertain flights of fancy of someone who may, in some aspects of human resumes, be more qualified."

"I mean…I knew that, I guess," I said slowly. "But it sounds like there's a level of understanding you might have that I don't. Or maybe it's just that voice in my head that I'll never advance in my career, never get promoted to a better, more prominent job."

"You say better, but it's in the way that…" Parthenope's expression became gentle. "This is a pressure of your society, isn't it?"

I shrugged. "My parents, mostly. Art is unreliable as income. A job at a small hotel would've been fine, but they expected more."

She made a contemplative sound. "Do you know why your predecessor retired?"

"Um…she never told me. I figured Patricia had gotten to an age where she wanted to do something else. I mean, this is more than a full-time job."

"In a sense. Patricia worked here since she was…well, she was probably not much older than you. So, my guess is she was here for about four decades. Patricia works now as an on-call mediator. It's much like humans who retire at a certain age but also continue keeping busy with a smaller job, one that is easier for them to handle," she explained. "But it's the forty years of experience at this hotel that allowed her to get that job. A human here learns on a need-to-know basis, but after decades, you reach a point where there is little you haven't needed to know. All the employees here respect our privacy as individuals, but they learn about us in general. Haven't you been learning like that?"

"Well, yeah," I admitted.

She gave me a small smile. "I'll gift you some knowledge here. My kind are at the hotel because we're searching for someone to make a child with." My lips parted and my eyes widened in surprise. "We're solitary by nature, we live our long lives alone for the most part, but to create a child requires us to find a mate. We won't stay together like humans do, I only come to meet with a group like this once every fifty years or more, but caring for our child will take sixteen months. Then they're old enough to be cared for by just one of us. If they were clever and cautious, they could even survive on their own."

I felt like I'd been trusted with a huge secret. "Wow. Thank you," I whispered. She smiled and nodded.

"So…when you say Patricia is a mediator, it's because she's a human who had, basically, an immersive education in nonhumans. And you call them when two…species, I guess is the word, come together after a conflict? Like when we had guests here who were going to the office complex for discussions?"

Parthenope's eyes brightened. "Exactly. And a human mediator has a huge amount of knowledge but also brings a unique perspective, which is why Patricia is so special. That's why I'm flabbergasted by how you see yourself." My eyebrows knitted together in confused curiosity. "This place, it's staggeringly important to all of us who visit. Maybe you've known it on an intellectual level, but you need to feel it, comprehend it. Appreciate it like we do.

"The worlds we navigate and the others who live there can be dangerous, malicious, and deadly, especially when you take into account ongoing wars, xenophobia, and vendettas. That includes our communities in other places on Earth. This can simply be a place we use as an intersection between planes, to know we can be ourselves, even if that calls for a disguise of a human form. But more than that, it is a place where we can retreat to when we feel as if we can't breathe, allowing us to step outside of our lives. Even if we live in the closest town."

"I've never heard any of the guests describe it like that," I said quietly. "But isn't that Mr. Lucero's job? He's the muscle behind the rules."

"Absolutely, but you, my dear Manager, are the hotel personified," Parthenope told me. "Cesar Lucero may be the force behind the crossroads, and the encyclopedia to which you turn when more knowledge is necessary to do your job, but his job is largely machinery that keeps everything running. You, though…you speak for him, you speak for the crossroads, and you speak for all of your guests. I would encourage you to be more attentive when you integrate yourself into confrontations, because you may be surprised what visible changes you notice in those involved.

"You work to arrange bargains that keep locals and visitors safe. You constantly speak to the employees to ensure we not only have what we need, whether it's sustenance or tools or comfort, but also your very presence makes us feel cared for. It makes us feel seen. And it reminds us of where we are, this special place, knowing we're in your hands."

I found myself, for the first time in a long time, choked up with happy tears. Averting my eyes, I blinked them back and took a deep breath. "I don't…" …*know what to say*.

"The standards you held yourself to have changed," she murmured. "You're part of our world now. And it was important that you understand how valuable your part is."

Swallowing hard, I nodded and looked back at Parthenope. "Well, thank you. I certainly do now," I whispered. She nodded her approval.

Chapter 9

I stopped in front of Nancy's desk and asked, "Do we have a PA system?"

Nancy looked up to me from the magazine she was reading and smirked. "You're asking about the music?"

"I mean…yeah."

Playing from nowhere that I could pinpoint was some sort of faint instrumental song, a live performance from a small orchestra that had some skill. My brain went through all references for familiar instruments and genres but couldn't place it. I was quite sure I already knew the answer to this question, which was that no, we didn't have a PA system, but of course I had to check.

"Paul told me it started around five," she said with a shrug. "It's Persian. You can hear the ney and the setar."

I stared incredulously. "How the hell did you know that?"

Nancy grinned. "One of the guests told me."

I rolled my eyes, and she chuckled as I walked to the front desk. The smell of breakfast wafted from the diner, and the murmurs of chatter could be faintly heard from everyone enjoying, or waiting for, their food. When I started my morning rounds in a few minutes, I was curious if I would hear the music playing in there also.

Josh was just settling in, taking a book out of the small backpack he brought with him. "Hey, what's with the music?" he asked. I repeated Nancy's explanation, but when he asked how I knew what instruments they were, I replied, "I'm just brilliant like that."

Josh looked in Nancy's direction and then toward the diner before saying, "One of the guests knew, didn't they?"

I stuck out my tongue at him and he smiled.

About half an hour later, a young man came walking in, spotting the reception desk, and smiled as he approached it. He was wearing a blue Polo shirt and tan slacks and had a small binder under his arms. He looked a few years older than me, maybe thirty, and had a can-do attitude about him. "Hi, I'm Kenneth Martin. I was hoping to speak with the owner."

My eyebrows rose in surprise, and I pushed myself to my feet. "The owner?"

"Yes. Mr. Cesar Lucero."

"Is he expecting you?"

I did not expect the answer to be in the affirmative. Firstly, the foyer with the door to Mr. Lucero's office has a separate entrance directly down a path from the parking lot, so this guy could've gone to ring that doorbell. Secondly, I've never been my boss's secretary. There's quite a bit of the business we collaborate on over the computer, but he fully handles quite a bit of it, because it falls under need-to-know.

So, coming up to the front desk meant Kenneth was just a solicitor of some sort. He was trying to pitch something. My curiosity was piqued, though, as to whether he knew what kind of hotel this was.

"No, I don't have an appointment, but I think he'll be interested in speaking to me," Kenneth replied.

"Why's that?"

"Like I said, business opportunity."

"Which is?"

Kenneth motioned to his binder. "I'm a marketing specialist for VTA, Vacation and Travel Association. We've been speaking with various hotels around the country, anyone for whom we'd believe it would be financially advantageous to set aside rooms for specific recurring customers, as timeshares."

I stood there for a moment, processing that. I considered saying, '*Don't you think someone who has run a hotel for a hundred and fifty years would've done this already if he wanted to?*'

Instead I said, "Guests."

He blinked, bemused. "Sorry?"

"They're not customers, if they're in the hotel. They're guests." I gestured with my hand to the hospitality sign, and his gaze went to it, taking a brief moment to skim it. Even if they had only come to the diner for a meal, I'd sometimes refer to our nonlocals as guests too, out of habit.

"Oh, of course," Kenneth said emphatically. He looked back at me. "My mistake. Guests. So, considering how *special* some of your guests are, they might be interested in locking down a timeshare. Many people of their standing would appreciate the assurance of knowing exactly where they'll be staying, and that it will be a hotel like the Crossroads. Knowing that their annual vacation is predictable, with no scheduling hassle, guaranteed to be available."

"Predictable," I said contemplatively. I slid my hands in my pockets, rocking back on my heels. "The guests of a certain standing, they're coming to this hotel for predictability?"

He seemed to have realized his gaffe despite my casual tone. It seemed he did indeed know a bit about the hotel. "Oh, of course there are always extenuating circumstances overall, but their room will be available. No need to go through the hassle of finding a place to stay."

"Right, the hassle. Because, 'predictable' isn't something we'd put in a slogan, if we decided to make one. Like, we don't have a PA system." I glanced pointedly around the room, listening to the music.

Kenneth did so too. "Ah. I see."

"If I may ask, are you *local,* or *nonlocal*?"

"I'm local, ma'am," he said with a knowing smile. "Grew up in Chicago, and I live in Connecticut now."

"Mm. So, what if…and I'm just positing a hypothetical…*another* guest of *some standing* would like a room, and I'm not able to give them an unused room because it's reserved? Even though no one is in it."

Kenneth shrugged. "That's unfortunate. But the numbers don't lie. Knowing the room is there and that they can count on it, that's important to these guests. So, it's an extremely good investment for a hotel."

It was clear he was convinced of his pitch, but I wondered exactly how new this company he worked for was. Annual profit or loss from the hotel wasn't an issue. I'd seen the books (at least the ones for human eyes, that sporadically had a few things we were paying for censored) and the hotel was doing fine. Mr. Lucero's prices were fair, but we *were* running a business, so we did make a good profit. You don't run a place for this long if you're often losing revenue.

The thing Kenneth had somehow gotten backwards was the priorities of those who stayed in the hotel, and therefore the priorities of the man who owned it. Timeshares, aside from being a cliché of a scam that prompted more searches online on how to get out of them than how to buy them, were for guaranteed rooms, yes. And maybe some of the haughtier of our guests would love to brag that they had a timeshare at The Crossroads.

But much more likely was that there would be very few who would go for it. Those who had unpredictable schedules, those who came for a meeting at the office complex, or if they visited for a convention like the one we were having now, they'd all be pissed. Maybe one percent of our guests would be interested in a timeshare, two percent if we were lucky.

There was also the ultimate short notice visit, when a guest was injured. That wasn't common, but it wasn't uncommon. And that wasn't a vacation; that was going to the place with rules, where whoever had hurt you couldn't follow. I couldn't imagine turning them away because a room was 'reserved'.

"See, that's where you lost me," I sighed, putting disappointment into my tone. "The idea that it's a good investment for the hotel. There are things we'll invest in for our guests, but we don't invest in things specifically for the purposes of making more profit. And certainly not at the risk of having fewer rooms available."

Kenneth narrowed his eyes, clearly not buying that. "Well…considering he's the owner, and this is his money we're talking about, I'd like to speak to Mr. Lucero anyway. Hear that straight from him."

"Oh, did you not see the sign directing you toward his office entrance?" I exclaimed, pointing back toward the parking lot. "Easy mistake."

That wasn't what he wanted to hear. Obviously, my boss had better things to do than listen to this guy's spiel, but if Kenneth could get me to give him a direct call, that might give the impression that it was worthwhile.

As if I'd call Mr. Lucero for something like this.

"Oh, I didn't want to be rude," he told me. "I was hoping you could call and make sure he had time for me rather than barge in. If not, we could schedule something for later."

"I see, I see. His schedule is rather busy, that's true," I agreed. Kenneth nodded once, smiling. "That's why I don't call him unless it's urgent and important. But I'll tell you what," I continued as his smile faded, picking up one of the business cards from the plastic holder on the counter, "why don't you send him an email?"

He took the card from me. "Email."

"Yup. You really seem to believe this would be good for the hotel, so why not write up exactly what all the benefits are, mention some numbers, and then he can make up his mind on his own?" He absently tucked the card away into his pocket. "After the conversation you and I had, you can even get out in front of some of the concerns he might have, the ones I mentioned."

This was a generous out for him, it was more than reasonable, but this was not an appealing option to Kenneth. Of course it wasn't. Selling timeshares to people required bribery to listen to them talk for hours; talking a hotel owner into making a change of this level meant a face-to-face conversation.

"Well…I-I think he-"

And there we go, I'm out of patience. "You know what?" I asked. "Why don't we ask the guests?"

"What?"

I started walking backwards. "Many of the women staying for a convention are down here for breakfast." Turning, I walked around from behind the desk, gesturing to him as I angled toward the diner. I had a quick glimpse of Josh's face as he stood up, revealing that he was clearly enjoying this entire spectacle. "Surely people who book the entire hotel for week-long events love it here, so they'd be interested in a timeshare."

Kenneth quickly caught up to me, keeping pace with me as I walked to the entrance of the diner. "I don't think Mr. Lucero would appreciate you proposing an investment-"

"Excuse me, everyone," I called out. There were only two tables of locals, and so when the room quieted around them (because of course it did, I'm the Manager), they stopped speaking and looked at me curiously. "There's a man here who thinks it would be a fantastic opportunity for both the hotel and its guests to set aside several rooms as timeshares," I said, my tone unmistakably genuine. "Would anyone currently staying here now be interested in that?"

There was only a brief moment where a couple of the women glanced around before every one of them burst out laughing.

"Hm," I said, biting my lip thoughtfully as I watched them laugh. Turning to Kenneth, I told him, "I don't think it's gonna work out." Sour-faced, he turned and walked away. "You can always email!"

As I watched the salesman leave out the front doors, I saw Josh chuckling. Turning back to the diner, I waved at the highly entertained guests, and then headed back to my desk.

The hours passed without any excitement, some of the guests coming and going, presumably to the swimming hole since they returned with wet hair. Luckily, the music we were stuck listening to was quite pleasant, and while we did get some questions about it from the guests, they seemed to shrug it off just as we did. When I asked, they said they couldn't hear it in their rooms, so it wasn't a real issue that might be annoying. In fact, one woman said it was lovely and reminded her of home.

None of the women came out to the lobby with their instruments, unsurprising so long as we still had the background music. The music faded away sometime around four in the afternoon, though I couldn't tell you exactly when.

I came back from my dinner break at about seven, and shortly after that, one of the guests approached me and Delilah. "Manager, can I ask a favor?" she asked.

Turning to face her, I asked, "Sure, what is it?"

"There's a woman at the bar who…is depressed," she explained gently. "I was hoping to have you join the conversation and perhaps offer her a room, because she wanted to ask permission to sleep in her car in the lot. I wanted to check with you first; I didn't mention the idea to her. Teles and I have been bonding, and I can take the other bed in her room." She made an awkward shrug. "I know that's a strange thing to say after the incident with that local the other day."

"It's actually refreshing," I told her as I stood up. "Having a local on the other end of the personality spectrum."

We walked into the diner and over to the bar. I had spotted the woman earlier, when I'd left the break room and exited through the kitchen doors to get back to my desk, but hadn't taken her in. She was white with her black hair in a cute pixie cut and looked to be somewhere in her thirties. She was dressed casually, with a green t-shirt and shorts and sneakers, and her face was red and blotchy, clearly revealing that she'd been crying.

"Cordelia," she said, drawing her attention, "this is the Manager, Marjorie."

"Oh, hi," Cordelia said, sitting up straighter. "Um, I was wondering-"

"She told me," I said with a comforting smile. "Is everything okay?"

The woman looked uncomfortable and shrugged. "Cheating husband."

My eyes widened. "Crap, I'm sorry. What happened? Did he kick you out?" I asked, taking a seat next to her.

"Oh no, nothing like that," she said dismissively. "I just- I told Kent what happened." She gestured to our bartender. "I was supposed to get on a flight to New York. But the flight was delayed, and delayed, and eventually they said, 'Hey, sorry, but we can't get you on a plane until tomorrow morning.'" Cordelia shook her head. "I had the flight for a business meeting tomorrow morning, so I called my boss and they just said they'd postpone it. I think we should just have it over Zoom, but what do I know?"

The woman sighed. "Anyway, I got home and I'm like, whose car is that in our driveway?"

"Oh," I said with a cringe.

"Yeah. I went in and they were on the living room couch with a bottle of wine." Cordelia looked back to her glass, which was almost empty of whatever she'd ordered. "They were tripping over each other's words, and she left pretty quick. I'm just grateful it wasn't later tonight, and I didn't come in and find them naked in our bed." I winced. "So, after a bit of yelling I went, hey, look, I'm already packed. Took my suitcase back out to the car and…drove off. It's not like he kicked me out, but even though I'm on the paperwork, it's his childhood home. I felt like telling him to leave would fall flat. It'd just be embarrassing."

She motioned with the glass. "If I'd gone to a local bar, the gossip would be across town by morning. So, after driving for a while, once I was all cried out, I pulled up Google Maps and found this place." Cordelia emptied her glass, let out another tired sigh, and glanced over to me. "But since you're fully booked and I plan on being too tipsy to drive, I was wondering if I could just hang out in the diner until it closes and then pass out in my car. I wanted to ask because I know that can look sketchy."

"A room just opened up, actually," I said with a small smile. "Two of the guests decided they'd like to share one of theirs that has two beds."

Cordelia blinked and looked to her right, at the woman who'd approached the desk. "Thel?" she asked.

Thelxinoe, that's her name!

"It's silly for you to sleep out there when there are beds in here," Thelxinoe told her. "Hospitality is quite

110

important to everyone who works at the Crossroads Hotel, and it's the biggest reason we chose this location for our week together. I'll gather my things, they'll put fresh sheets on the bed, and you'll have a good night's sleep. Then tomorrow, you can join us for breakfast. And you need to have dinner, especially if you want to continue drinking. The best part of that is, there's no better food within a hundred miles."

"That's...so nice of you," she said, looking shocked. "Thank you." Thelxinoe nodded once.

"If you want a distraction, maybe break out the board games again?" I suggested to Thelxinoe.

Her eyes brightened and she looked to Cordelia. "Do you play Scrabble?"

"Um...yeah, but I'm kind of crap at it," she admitted.

"That's even better," Thelxinoe said cheerfully. Cordelia smiled and chuckled.

Getting on the walkie, I called up Fyfe as I watched Thelxinoe, accompanied by Teles, go to get her things and move rooms. I asked him to please turn over the room for Cordelia, and then had her come to the front desk and check in on the computer and the ledger. I gave Delilah a brief summary of what was going on, deciding to wait until after Cordelia had gone back to the bar to give my coworker the more personal background info.

"As Thelxinoe said, the food here is great," I told her. "Order whatever is your favorite, have a few more drinks, and forget about that asshole by enjoying the fact that all the guests here right now are women."

Cordelia laughed. "Yeah, good point. Thanks again, this is so kind, you and Thel. I didn't want to be a bother," she said. Her eyes went to the diner briefly and she looked a little guilty.

"Look, a guy marched in here recently demanding a room and yelled at me so much, I cried," I told her quietly, drawing her gaze, which turned surprised. "Not to mention, last week two guys came in here with guns to empty the registers."

"Jesus," she breathed.

"Yeah. And that practically never happens here. I'm kind of just happy we got something to balance it out," I said, easing myself back into my comfy rolling chair. "To remind me that not all locals are arrogant jerks. And having one of the guests extend some kindness helped me remember that I do like this part of my job. It's on the wall and everything."

She followed my gesture and looked over the hospitality sign, staring thoughtfully as she read it before nodding. "That makes sense. And…it sounds like it makes this a pretty great place to work."

I gave her a genuine smile. "It is."

Chapter 10

There was nothing on my phone when I woke up the next morning, which made me smile. I would read over Carl's notes to see if anything occurred overnight, I always did. But there was nothing urgent from him or Paul, and that was always a good way to start the day.

Per usual, Josh beat me to the front desk, and I filled him in on the surprising fact that we actually had a new guest. Once I'd done my morning check-ins around the hotel, he presented me with a book he'd mentioned, Let's Pretend This Never Happened by Jenny Lawson. He had described it as 'the funniest and weirdest' biographical book he'd ever read and said that I would love it. I handed over my sketchbook to him, trading him for the book, and we both started on our respective ways to pass the time.

But after a few minutes of muffled chuckling as I read the first few pages, I finally cracked up laughing and put the book aside on the table. "I cannot read this right now."

"What? Why?" Josh asked, dismayed, looking up from my sketchpad. "I've barely had time to get started."

"It's hilarious, and it's just the first chapter! I'm going be crying with laughter, and everyone's going to stare at me," I told him. "But it seems fantastic, thank you. I'm stealing it, and I'll start reading it tonight."

Josh smiled back at me. "Just wait until you get to the part about the turkeys. Oh my god."

I shook my head. "I have no idea what that means, but I look forward to finding out. I didn't give you much time. What'd you come up with?"

"Hey, I'm not done," he said sternly.

I pursed my lips in amusement as he diligently resumed his work, then took out my phone and leaned back in my chair. Pulling up Reddit, I killed some time scrolling through my feed. Once another few minutes had passed, he spoke up, pulling my attention back to him. "All right. That's good enough."

Turning the sketchpad around, I saw two stick figures behind a reception desk, two more standing on the other side, and they were looking down at one on the floor. His tongue was sticking out and he had x's for eyes.

I burst out laughing. "Holy crap, it looks like he's dead! He just passed out, for like, three seconds!"

Josh made a sound of irritation, turning it back to give it a once over. "Yeah, but I didn't know how else to make him look ridiculous and half conscious."

"It's still brilliant," I told him.

He smiled and passed it back over. "Hey, so, I don't know if this is weird, but my mom keeps bugging me about it, since we sit here all day. Could you…draw me?"

My eyebrows rose. "Your mom keeps bugging you?"

"Well yeah, I've told her how awesome an artist you are," he said, shrugging, "I mention the latest and greatest stuff you show me, so now she wants a picture of me. She's like, 'You're sitting next to her the whole time you're there! I want a beautiful picture of my boy!' I'm just wondering how much you'd charge."

"How much-" I laughed suddenly and picked up the sketchpad, holding it out to him. "Dude, take your pick."

"What?" Josh took the sketchpad from me. "You already- Am I in here?"

"I sit next to you all day," I echoed emphatically. "I just never show anyone that stuff, cause it can get so awkward. One person thinks it's weird, one person thinks I made their nose too big, one person's like, 'Oh my god, do you really think I'm that pretty?'" I shook my head. "And I'm always self-conscious when it's a friend. Practicing on live subjects is great, but I don't show them the final product."

Josh absorbed this thoughtfully before becoming indignant and asking, "What about the guest drawing you did? The one you *cremated*? You went to great pains to tell him you couldn't help but draw something so gorgeous, and that he could obviously do what he wished with it."

I glared at him. "Are you really comparing yourself to a wolf?"

He dropped the faux annoyance with comedic swiftness, replying, "Of course not." Opening the book, he flipped through, making a few interested facial expressions at various sketches, until he found one of him. "Wow. Oh…holy shit, girl," he said, grinning at me before looking back to the drawing. "This is awesome."

"I've done three. You can take them all," I said, gesturing vaguely. "Your mom will be psyched."

He glanced at me in surprise before looking for the others. "This is so cool…" Josh leaned back in his chair. "If I give her all three, she's going to-" He let out a breath through his nose. "She's my mother, and doesn't care that you're technically my boss. I'm sitting next to a girl all day, who drew three gorgeous pictures of me."

"*Oh*," I said, leaning on my right armrest. Josh was absolutely one of my best friends at this point, but there was nothing between us. Which, honestly, I was incredibly grateful for. The last thing I needed right now, amidst the mess that I already was, was to catch feelings for the coworker I sat at the desk with for eight hours a day. "Gotcha. Alright, just choose your favorite, then."

Josh coughed out a laugh. "My favorite?" He looked down to the sketchbook, flipping back and forth between them. "Sometimes I think you really don't know how good you are."

"Of course I know," I said dismissively. "Otherwise, I wouldn't be able to pay for a whole room full of art supplies from what I sell. My salary here is great, but I seriously spoil myself shopping for that stuff."

Josh smiled to himself, pausing as he looked back and forth, before deciding on one. Carefully bending the page along the perforated line and then again in the other direction, he slowly pulled it out from the book.

Then he closed the sketchbook and handed it back. "You rock."

"Thank you."

I went back to occupying myself with my phone, hopping over to Pinterest for a bit, before tucking it back into my pocket and picking up my pencil.

It felt like a nonspecific sort of day. Letting my mind drift, I just sketched some of the items on the reception desk, putting more effort into capturing the way the light hit them and the shadows they formed. Eventually I fell into doing an old favorite of mine from school, drawing my hand as it drew my hand. I'd once gone a level deeper, having that hand drawing a hand, which for some reason had highly amused me.

I think I'd been in math class at the time though, and my teacher had pointedly asked me if I knew the answer to something she'd been explaining. It will not surprise you that I hadn't known.

People came and went, from the hotel and the diner, in my peripheral vision. Eventually I saw someone walk up to the side of the desk and I looked up as she spoke, "Excuse me."

I smiled. "Cordelia. How you doing?"

"I'm good," she said, nodding, shifting her purse on her shoulder. "Last night was really fun, actually, everyone was so nice. They broke out the Scrabble board, I had some drinks. I had dinner first, and oh my god, that country fried steak was the best."

"There is one thing I can always count on in my world, and it's that our diner serves good food," I said solemnly.

"Agreed. Anyway, Teles and a couple of the other women invited me to the swimming hole, but of course, I don't have a swimsuit with me. They said there's basically only one place to buy one here, across the street?"

I nodded. "This and That. It doesn't have a big clothing selection, but it has enough. And it actually has a surprisingly decent bathing suit selection, but I think that's because some guests find out about the swimming hole after they arrive."

"Gotcha," she said with a nod. "Also…do you happen to know if Ligeia is… I mean, I'm still married, but after what happened, I…" She winced, looking embarrassed. "Is she seeing anyone?"

"I'm not the person to ask, really," I said with a small smile. "I met everyone for the first time on Sunday. But I haven't seen her hanging out with any of the other guests in particular."

"Okay. Well, thanks again for the room last night. I slept really well."

"No problem," I replied. She gave me a smile before heading off.

I went back to my sketchbook, continuing what probably just qualified as doodling. But half an hour or so later, I was distracted from my usual focus and shifted in my seat, looking up and around. It felt too warm, like the air conditioning had been turned off and we were starting to feel it. Except I still heard the humming of the system going.

"Do you feel warm?" I asked Josh.

"Hm?" He looked up from his book, thought for a moment, and then his eyes narrowed. "Yeah. A/C problems?"

Putting aside my sketchpad and shaking my head, I stood up, unclipping my walkie from my belt. "Let me ask." I turned to channel two and pressed the button to speak into it as I walked out from behind the desk. "Marjorie for Fyfe."

"Go for Fyfe."

"The lobby's feeling a bit warm. Anything going on with the air conditioning? Over." I arrived at the thermostat on the wall, which revealed it was indeed getting into the eighties.

There was only a brief pause. "I'm up in room twelve, and it feels fine. Let me do some checking, I'll get back to you. Over."

"Thanks. Marjorie out."

I walked back to the front desk, turning the walkie back to channel one before putting it down on the counter. "Thermostat agrees with us. Fyfe says room twelve is still getting A/C."

"That's weird, considering heat rises," Josh noted.

Chuckling, I told him, "If it's weird, then it'll likely resolve itself, considering where we work. Which is better than an actual problem, because I really don't want to have an issue with the A/C system in the middle of summer."

Josh made a small noise of agreement, taking out his phone. Presumably he was going to check on the weather, but no matter what it told us, it wouldn't help if we had a hotel problem, typical or atypical.

Jodie came to the threshold of the diner and caught my attention. "Hey, Marjorie?"

"If it's about the A/C, we're on it," I called back. She smiled and gave a wave of thanks before going back in.

After a few minutes, Fyfe spoke over the walkie. "Fyfe for Marjorie, I don't see any system issues. Over."

I groaned quietly before answering. "Not my area, but the thermostat on the wall over here agrees with us. Can you try to compensate? Over."

"Yeah, lass, can do. The thermostat I've got here agrees with yours, despite the fact that it's still doing its job. I'll pull it down a few degrees. Update me on any changes. Over."

Unfortunately, as the minutes passed, there were no changes. At least none that were discernible to me and Josh, but when I checked the thermostat fifteen minutes later, it was actually two degrees higher. Sighing and hoping the problem would resolve on its own eventually, I just went back to business as usual. We'd passed the lunch rush, at least, so there weren't too many people there who could complain. And our guests would probably just take the opportunity to hang out in their tubs.

"Okay, now I'm worried," Josh said, his tone emphasizing his feelings.

I looked up to him and followed his gaze, realizing that the air in the hotel was getting misty. "What the hell?"

"Has this ever happened before?"

"Not in my time here," I said, turning back to him. He had pulled his knees up and had his feet on his chair. "What on Earth are you doing?" I glanced down briefly. "Did you see a mouse?"

"No, but I've seen this movie, and I'll probably die first," he told me.

I chuckled, getting to my feet. "Oh, for crying out loud. Nobody's dying," I said, leaving to go to the sundry shop.

"Yeah, you say that now. Just wait until a tentacle pulls you out of the hotel," he called after me.

Grinning, I walked over to Nancy, who shrugged as I arrived. "No clue," she answered, not even needing the question. "Never happened before."

"Great," I sighed.

Heading back to the front desk as the fog started to get thicker, I shook my head. Most strange stuff was irritating, but this was something that could genuinely freak out the guests. *Thanks a lot, Stephen King.*

Josh had put his feet back on the floor but still looked concerned. "Well?"

"First time."

"Fantastic."

Having built up enough to obscure the entrance to the diner, I only noticed Andrea walking toward me when she got closer. She didn't say a word, just stopped in front of the counter, cocking her head expectantly.

"If it's a safety hazard cooking in the kitchen, just take a break," I told her. "As my slogan goes, I do not control the hotel. Just tell any locals that it's an issue with the A/C, nothing bad, just…condensation…stuff."

Letting out a breath through her nose, Andrea wordlessly spun on a heel and went back the way she'd come. I chuckled; I couldn't help it. We seldom had issues that bordered on horror-movie territory. Some of it was annoying, some it was great, and some of it was hilarious (in hindsight). Even so, this only made me curious.

"You're the one with all the book learnin' from your binge reading," I said, glancing at Josh. "Why would we be getting fog?"

"Hey, you went to college," he responded, though he visibly started thinking about my question. "I'm just a nerdy bookworm." He absorbed the question and then furrowed his eyebrows. "Hot air over cold air. I mean, that's why you often see fog on lakes and stuff, because it could be humid out the water…" Josh sighed. "It *is* the A/C."

"What?"

"We're getting weather from somewhere else, and fighting it with cold air," he said, looking at me in exasperation. "The more we fight it, the worse the fog gets."

I rolled my eyes. "Great. So, what, we either keep it in the eighties or we're able to see more than a dozen feet in front of us?"

Josh gestured helplessly. "Don't hate the player, hate the science."

Shaking my head, I smiled, picking up the walkie. "Well, I asked. You answered. I'll tell Fyfe and Andrea."

"Tell me what?" the chef asked, popping up suddenly from the other side of the counter.

Josh startled and gasped, but I am ashamed to admit that I actually shrieked.

"Oh my god!" I exclaimed as Andrea started cackling. "What is wrong with you?"

"I can't do my damn job," she told me with a grin. "You take away my toys, I get bored."

I relented, laughing as my heartbeat slowed to normal, and jabbed a finger at the kitchen. "Go bother someone else."

"Yes, boss, right away, boss," she said, saluting before she walked away.

"A coworker, not a guest!" I clarified after her. She just laughed.

Thankfully, the invasive weather faded after about an hour, and none of the people in the diner left because of it. I spent some time thinking about how to startle Andrea.

After all, I know what time she gets back for her second shift later, and Giovanna and Patrick will know which cabinets or pantries she might open first.

The Crossroads Hotel: Volume 2

Chapter 11

With bacon and eggs sizzling in their respective pans, Andrea cracked two more eggs one-handed into a bowl before grabbing the tongs and flipping over the bacon. Then she took the whisk from where she'd left it and started scrambling the eggs, but was distracted by the walkie talkie on her waist.

"Marjorie for Andrea."

She glanced at Giovanna, who was putting some French toast into a pan. "Hey, take over for me?" she asked.

"Sure thing, boss."

The chef took a few steps away from the stove, picking up her walkie. "Go for Andrea."

"I've got a favor to ask." Marjorie sounded hurried, and Andrea's eyebrows went up in interest as she glanced at the clock. It was only 8:15 a.m., and the Manager's shift didn't start for another forty-five minutes. "There's a guest who's coming in with a question about an event, short notice. Food questions. I'm paranoid they'll be waiting in the lobby before I'm downstairs. Can you just hang out there until I get there? Over."

"Sure thing," she replied, starting to walk toward the doors that led to the diner. Andrea gave a nod to the other cook, Patrick, who had overheard as she said, "See you soon. Over."

"Thanks. Marjorie out."

Leaving the kitchen and walking out past the guests having their breakfast, Andrea walked into the lobby and gave a wave to Carl. "Hey."

"Hey yourself," the older man said with a smile. "To what do I owe the pleasure?"

"Just waiting for Marjorie," she replied, leaning on the counter. "New guest might beat her to the lobby and it's food related. Anything exciting happen last night?"

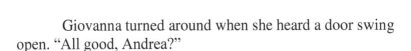

Giovanna turned around when she heard a door swing open. "All good, Andrea?"

"Yeah, false alarm, Carl's got it." The woman walked to the wide window that opened to the dining room, where order notes were placed. "Back to work."

Patrick looked over. "Jodie said someone just put in an order for an omelette."

"Oooh," she muttered. Picking up one of two tickets, she smiled. "Indeed. And they have good taste, which is always nice. Tempted to make another for myself."

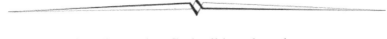

Andrea listened to Carl tell her about how someone with insomnia had come out to hang out in the lobby with their lyre the previous night and nearly put him to sleep with the calm, beautiful music. Also, he mentioned several calls he'd gotten, something that was more common than one would think. Since the Crossroads received calls from all manner of time zones, it might be 3 a.m. in Missouri when someone called on their lunch break on the other side of the planet.

Then Andrea learned that, apparently, they'd gotten some more music from nowhere for two hours or so. Carl described it as a duet of a string instrument and a wind instrument, but he had no idea what kinds. Gratefully, whoever the musicians were, they kept up a quicker beat and engaging tune instead of tempting him into taking a nap, and he enjoyed it in the background while he read a book.

Once she felt like taking a load off, Andrea walked over to the couches, sitting down into the comfy cushions. It was nice to rest, but the breakfast rush had just started, and she would rather have been in the kitchen. It would've been better if this had happened in a few hours, but of course, she didn't get to choose these things. She took out her phone and checked her email, then spent some time hopping around a few apps, and then tucked it away with a sigh.

At about 8:45, Josh wandered in and gave her a curious wave. She returned it, then resumed tapping her fingers against her leg, her mind wandering. Finally, about five minutes later, the stairwell door on the far side of the lobby opened and Marjorie walked out.

I walked into the lobby, spotting Andrea on the couch. "Hey, about time," she sighed, pushing herself to her feet. "This is my morning fun time you're cutting into."

"Oh, I'm sorry," I said, becoming mildly flustered. "Did I miss a note in the app? What's up?"

Andrea cocked an eyebrow. "What's up? The guest. The one with the food questions."

I wracked my brain for a few seconds, trying to recall a conversation we'd possibly had in the last few days, before shaking my head. "I don't remember."

Narrowing her eyes suspiciously, the chef stared at me for a long moment before asking, "Did you call me on the walkie like half an hour ago?"

That surprised me. "What? No. What do you mean-"

Andrea let out an annoyed growl. Spinning on a heel, she marched back toward the diner, and I was instinctively right on her heels. "Puck!" she yelled in incensed annoyance. Everyone in the diner glanced at her, startled, and I wondered if she'd gotten one letter wrong in that word.

Shoving both swinging doors open without a warning, since a warning had already been clearly shouted, Andrea stormed into the kitchen. I darted in after her, scanning the room, only seeing Patrick and Giovanna. But both of them looked mildly irritated.

"Where is he?"

"*She* heard you yell, so she said, 'That's my cue,' and went into the walk-in," Patrick said tiredly, pointing in its direction.

Andrea bolted over and swung the door open. "Not cool, asshole!" she bellowed into the empty freezer. "Stay out of my *kitchen!*"

Slamming the door shut with a huff, Andrea looked to her cooks. "What did he make?"

"Breakfast food," Giovanna said, shrugging. "Started with an omelette, then I think ham and grits, there was bacon, toast-"

"Toast! Shit," Andrea snapped, going quickly to one of the cabinets. I saw Patrick take a few steps to the fridge, opening the door.

"All right, what is going on? Please?" I asked, folding my arms.

Andrea threw up her hands. "He took two loaves."

"Yeah, we're out a gallon of milk," Patrick sighed, shutting the door. He went back to the order he'd been working on, as did Giovanna.

I shifted my weight from one foot to another. "So, someone cooked our guests some food, then stole some. Would anyone care to tell me who he is?" I asked. "Who she is?"

Rubbing her hands over her face, Andrea muttered something too quietly for me to hear before answering, "He's fae. Not dangerous, just annoying. He's done this before. Distracted me, marched into the kitchen looking like me, and started cooking. He likes to cook for our guests, it probably makes him feel special working in the Crossroads kitchen, and it's absolutely his type of thing, because he's a trickster."

"A tricker," I stated. "Like Loki?"

Andrea smirked. "Fuck, I'd be a lot more worried if we got a visit from the god himself. The stuff he might try to pull would probably violate hospitality in five different ways."

Patrick glanced back at me. "They're under the same general shapeshifter umbrella," he explained. "Puck just doesn't have a kid who's a wolf that's supposed to cause an apocalypse or one that's a serpent the size of a planet, and Puck never fucked a horse and got pregnant."

After staring at Patrick for a long moment, I said, "You know, information is important as the Manager of this hotel, but there are some things that I don't need to know."

Chuckling, Andrea shook her head. "Honestly, it's just wildly aggravating. If Vesta graces us with her presence every few years to ask if she can bake a few loaves of bread, I am rolling out the red carpet for her," she said with a gesture. "If Puck wanted to cook for us, because he *is* a good cook, it'd be fine if he asked. But instead, he walks in like he owns the place, does what he wants, then takes bread and milk as payment."

"Because he finds it hilarious," I said with a small smile. "I mean…it kind of is. Just like it was hilarious when you scared the shit out of me yesterday in the lobby. Think this might have just been karma?" Andrea scowled at me. Muffling a chuckle that bubbled up inside me, I asked, "All right, I'll shift gears. Anything to report?"

"No, no, we're good, breakfast rush is good," Andrea told me, motioning around vaguely with a hand. "All the food will be tasty despite the unwelcome intruder who cooked it. Now, get out so I can pretend I'm in control of my kitchen."

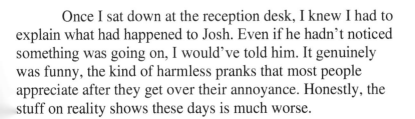

Once I sat down at the reception desk, I knew I had to explain what had happened to Josh. Even if he hadn't noticed something was going on, I would've told him. It genuinely was funny, the kind of harmless pranks that most people appreciate after they get over their annoyance. Honestly, the stuff on reality shows these days is much worse.

I wonder if Loki's in Hollywood these days, producing terrifying prank shows…

Also, Josh let me know that his mother was over the moon with the drawing I'd done of him. He told me not to be surprised if she asked for one of his brother, or someone else in the family, or even a family photo. I replied that, of course, I'd be delighted to sketch anything her heart desired.

Morning eventually became afternoon, and I brought my lunch back to my desk, since at some point Josh and I had somehow gotten engaged in a really interesting conversation about Norse mythology. He discussed the stories about Loki, since once Patrick had told me about the trickster's children like a title for a clickbait article, I felt compelled to learn more about him. My coworker knew an impressive amount about the stories, which was unsurprising considering how entertaining they were.

About an hour later, a man walked into the hotel, which always prompted me to glance up. He was Indian, with dark skin and a graying goatee, wearing a pale button-up shirt and faded jeans. I heard the lyre music from one of the women in the lobby trail off, and realized they'd taken note of him as well.

What really caught my attention were the two dogs with him, which prompted me to smile and sit up a little straighter. I was still hoping for an opportunity to hang out with a puppy in the near future. These two looked like some kind of boxer mix, with a beautiful red and brown mottled pattern of short fur.

The man also smiled as he noticed me, leisurely walking over, each dog keeping perfect pace beside him. "Hello," he said, glancing at my name tag with open curiosity as I stood up. "Marjorie. You're the new manager? I'm afraid it's been some time since I've visited the hotel."

"I am," I replied with a welcoming smile. "Patricia retired two years ago, and I took over. Though I'm under the impression she's not exactly off doing pool yoga or playing pickleball."

"Yoga in the pool?" His eyes widened in surprise. "I hadn't heard of such a thing before. Or pickleball."

"It's pretty new, I think. As for pickleball…" I let out a breath. "I…don't actually know what that is, now that I think about it," I remarked. "Maybe when we turn sixty, we get a booklet in the mail that tells us. And gives us strategies for getting all the best senior discounts."

He chuckled. "Perhaps." He gave me a nod that was more of a bow as he said, "It's nice to meet you, Marjorie. I was hoping to have a meal, but I know my dogs aren't allowed in the diner. Would it be possible to order and eat in the lobby?"

"Of course," I said. "You can have a seat and I'll let the kitchen know to send someone out."

"Thank you." He walked over toward the couches and tables.

There were several guests there who were watching the man somewhat warily, but among them was Cordelia who quietly went, "Puppies! Hi!" which prompted me to grin. If I hadn't been working, I'd have been over there in a heartbeat doing the same thing.

The man spoke a word in another language, and that seemed to be the command allowing the dogs to leave his side. "They're quite friendly," he said as he took a seat, watching them go over to the woman who was clearly enamored with them. In my experience, dogs never failed to spot and make a beeline for the people who were eager to pat them.

"Can you give the kitchen a call?" I asked, glancing at Josh, who'd watched the interaction. I was always looking for opportunities to let him do things that involved nonlocal guests. He'd give a description of the guest, since it was likely someone there would recognize him, and possibly start prepping for the food he liked to order.

"Will do." He then nodded his head in their direction with a knowing smile. "Come on, go pat the dang dogs."

I laughed and relented, walking out from behind the counter as he picked up the phone. Heading over to the couches and loveseats, I took a seat nearby, saying, "Hey sweeties," and one of them left Cordelia's side to trot over to me. Two hands were better than one, after all.

A few moments later, my eyebrows rose when I heard Nancy speak up behind me. "It's been a while." I continued to give the dog scritches behind her ear as I turned and saw Nancy just a few feet away, having walked over from the sundry shop, her hands in her pockets.

"It has," the man replied. "But I found myself craving Andrea's cooking. Oh, she is still here, isn't she?"

She nodded. "Oh yeah, she is." She paused before asking, "Any…reason for your visit?"

That was peculiar. Nancy seldom left the sundry shop to greet guests, and asking them about any business they had here was strange. Or at least, I would say it was unusual, and I myself would have felt rude doing it. Typically, the guests' privacy is respected in those areas, by 'those areas' I mean the purpose of their visit and who they really are. Sometimes they'll pay cash (or a currency substitute) at the diner and leave without us even knowing their first name.

Glancing at the guests, I noticed they were attentive to the exchange. That made me even more curious.

"It's…hard to say," he spoke thoughtfully. "Which is a bit strange." He paused before continuing, "Mostly I'm looking forward to giving Andrea something to cook for me."

A smile spread across Nancy's face. "That's not uncommon. And when she hears you're visiting, she'll be just as happy to be getting that order from you." The man returned the smile before Nancy walked back to the shop, and just as she did so, Jodie came out from the diner.

"Hey there," she said with a friendly grin, her pad of paper and pen in her hand. "What can I get for you today?" she asked.

"I'd like idiyappam, please, with curry. Chef's choice. No drink."

Jodie wrote it down and nodded. "Coming right up," she said before turning and heading to the kitchen. The man pulled the coffee table a foot closer to the loveseat he was in.

"Do you have a favorite dish you've ordered more than once?" I asked, continuing to pat the dog next to me, my fingernails running up and down her back. She put her chin on my knee, blinking once languidly.

"Ah, never," he said with a shake of his head. "Always something different. And your chef is always delighted with my feedback, whether I give a critique for the future or tell her it was perfect and not to change a thing."

I nodded slowly. That was very like Andrea. "It was nice to meet you," I told the dog softly, leaning down toward her face. Her tail wagged and her eyes looked to mine before giving me a lick on my nose. I squinted and grinned. "Thank you."

I stood up and gave a departing wave to the guests, who seemed to be more at ease now, and walked back behind the desk. "Are you a curry person?" I asked Josh. "I've had it on occasion, but it was never a staple of my diet."

"Oh yeah, my dad's a pretty big fan of Indian food," he replied. "We'll usually have something every few weeks. But we'll eat out, because as good as my mom is, some of the best stuff takes a long time to prep." Josh paused, glancing toward the diner. "But now you've got me craving curry."

"I'm sure Andrea would be happy to make another one for you," I replied. "And…maybe one for me too. Seems the craving is contagious."

"All the best ones are."

Glancing back to the man and his dogs, I took out my cell, leaning forward on the upper reception counter. Typing out a message, I sent it to Nancy, looking to my right toward the far side of the room, watching as she heard the notification and took her phone from her pocket.

What was that about?

Nancy glanced up to me, then back to her phone. She looked at my message for a long moment before replying.

Sometimes guests don't have actual business here. Sometimes they're drawn to atmospheres where certain things are happening, or will happen. Things that are in their wheelhouse.

That was, while vague, a fascinating concept. I wondered if there had been correlations between unusual things happening in the hotel and a visitor we'd received, but that I hadn't noticed because I hadn't been paying attention.

Though I was far from an expert, and so probably wouldn't have realized a correlation anyway. However, it framed the coincidence of Puck messing with Andrea in a whole different light. Maybe his visit *had* been a sort of karma.

Considering Nancy had worked here for so long, though, and probably knew who the man was if she was so bold as to ask a question of him, she may have been here at a time when his visit heralded something. He'd taken the question in stride, after all, as if he'd expected it.

Not even sure if she'd tell me, I asked, *What's in his wheelhouse?*

Surprisingly, she didn't hesitate that much. I guess when I was audacious enough to ask these questions, I would sometimes get answers.

Last time he was here was something like five years ago. He said he was going to stay at the hotel for work. Two days later, one of the guests died in their sleep. He left that morning.

I looked up to Nancy worriedly, and she gave a sad grimace. So, this guy could be a literal death omen. But from what he had said, it wasn't that straightforward this time; it was hard to say. Maybe someone was dying, close to death, and didn't know it. Like they had progressive cancer or something similar.

Or maybe it was me. I looked at the man and his dogs, the latter still getting spoiled with pats and scritches, now from the sirens as well. I wouldn't have been surprised if he was confused because there was a dead person running the hotel now. Sighing, I wondered how often this would happen. How frequently my 'condition' would be relevant to conversations. I didn't see it magically ending even after I'd fully come to terms with it on a psychological level.

I gave Nancy a nod, tucking away my phone. At least, unlike food cravings, being dead wasn't contagious. This job was quite enjoyable overall, and I'd have hated to have a hazmat suit be my mandatory attire.

Chapter 12

The next day, I was doing some accounting work on the computer when a woman walked in and approached the reception desk. I looked up and smiled in recognition. "Hey, you're back." She was a Hispanic woman with striking dark brown eyes, her long brown hair tied back in a scrunchie, and her name was Laila. She'd stayed at the hotel for just one night the previous week and, on the scale of being a local, was perfectly polite.

"I am back, but just for a minute," she said with a tight smile. "I called last night because I realized I forgot a book here. No idea how I managed that. I just needed to find the time to drive over, but the woman I spoke to said that she was sure it would be in your lost and found."

"Absolutely," I replied, pointing toward the sundry shop. "You can tell Nancy."

"Great, thank you," Laila said, nodding once before heading over.

Like many things here, the lost and found for the hotel was next level. Anything Fyfe found in rooms or around the hotel, anything left in the diner, even something found on the roof, it all went to lost and found. That meant it was given to Nancy, who put it in Storage. Whatever was behind that mysterious door, there was apparently also an impressive amount of spare space.

Laila's book was indeed there and she gave me a wave of thanks before she left.

Nancy told me that they kept things in lost and found indefinitely, they always had, and when I had cocked an eyebrow in disbelief, she just nodded. The hotel had been open for at least a century and a half, so that meant an absolute ton of random stuff. But considering the guests who stayed with us, I supposed it made sense. I had learned time can do wonky things with people who visited the hotel if they existed on another plane. Not to mention, if it *was* something that belonged to someone nonlocal, it could be important in a way we couldn't understand.

Still, I had this image of a giant box full of nothing but ordinary cell phone chargers on a shelf in there, left to gather dust until the end of time.

About an hour later, I was sitting in my chair when, without any warning or discernible cause, a pang of panic hit me. It felt as if there was cause for alarm, like the jolt of adrenaline from being in a dark room, seeing a bathrobe on the back of a door, and thinking there was an intruder. My pencil twitched, making a jagged scribble, and I narrowed my eyes in concern. Looking over to Josh, he was still steadfastly reading his book and only looked up when I asked, "Did you feel that?"

He hesitated, absorbing the question. In this place, it could be nothing, or it could be everything. "Feel what?" he finally asked, the inevitable reply.

"Just, like, a chill," I told him. "I don't know."

"Like something's up?"

I pursed my lips. "Maybe. Do you ever get that feeling with ghosts?"

He shook his head. "Nope. Even the jerks couldn't so much as nudge a balloon. There was never any sensation, so I could just walk right through them, which was actually kinda funny," he smirked. "There's really not much they can do, and it was the most obnoxious way I could tell them to go screw themselves."

Movement caught my attention as I saw Cordelia walk quickly past the front desk, hands shoved in her pockets, and out the front doors.

"Maybe it's nothing," I said, knowing I was jinxing myself. "Or maybe it's like that thing where you're sleeping, and you suddenly feel like you're falling so you startle awake. You think that can happen when I'm awake, now that I'm dead?"

Josh chuckled. "I sure hope not. That would be really annoying. If it happened randomly, in the middle of a conversation or something.

Just then I heard a door open, recognizable to me as the door to Storage, with such force that it hit the wall before bouncing back to gradually close on the automatic hinge. It prompted me to jump to my feet in concern and lean over the counter to look toward the sundry shop.

"Nancy, with me," Mr. Lucero snapped.

I narrowed my eyes. "What's going on?" I asked, straightening as he speed-walked over to the front desk, Nancy quick on his heels. Her expression was alarmed, and it looked like she was scanning the area to become more aware of her surroundings, as if there might be trouble. I'd never seen her do that before.

My boss put his hands flat on the counter, stone-faced as he met my gaze. "Someone was just attacked on hotel grounds."

I took a sharp breath as I heard Josh stand up behind me. "Is that what that feeling was? What happened?"

He furrowed his eyebrows. "You felt it? That's impressive. I don't know exactly what happened yet, only what I felt," he said, rubbing his sternum. I got the feeling that whatever sensation he'd gotten, as a wizard and being the official guardian in charge of the crossroads, had been a lot more forceful. "Did anything out of the ordinary just happen? Any sign of where the attack could have occurred?"

My mouth opened as I mentally rewound the past few minutes, but my train of thought was interrupted when I heard a car start outside. "Cordelia. She just left," I said, already running out from behind the desk. Leaving Josh to keep an eye on things, I hurried after Mr. Lucero and Nancy, and we got outside just in time to see Cordelia speed out of the parking lot. We just stood there and watched her leave.

I looked at Mr. Lucero, my expression serious. "When you said attacked, do you mean fatally?" I asked.

"It was an attempted murder. Whether she was successful or not is yet to be determined." His eyebrows twitched thoughtfully before he was moving again. My coworker and I followed as he walked across the lot and out into the middle of the street, watching her car speed away in the distance. He remained quiet as it went, standing in the middle of that lane as Nancy and I remained just short of the road's threshold.

A car came from the other direction, and I waited as it passed. "What do we do?" I asked.

"We're doing it." He continued staring until the car was out of sight, then slowly turned around to face the opposite direction. "The crossroads is locked down. No one in or out."

Realizing what that meant, my eyes darted in the direction he was looking and then back to him, mildly distressed. "Is that the best place to be standing?"

"It is. But in a minute." Mr. Lucero walked off the pavement and onto the grass, looking back toward Nancy. "If you'd be so kind? This is going to get exciting."

"Yeah, I bet." At that, she reached into her pocket and took out a wand.

My eyes widened. *Well. This is new.*

Nancy's expression was hard to read, though it was apparent she was angry. I saw her mutter something under her breath and make a gesture with her wand. But nothing happened that was visible to me. Falling into an anxious silence, I shifted uneasily on my feet. We waited, an occasional car passing by.

About a minute later I heard the car in the distance coming from the east, identifiable from the volume of its velocity, and when it came into view, Mr. Lucero walked into the middle of the lane. I swallowed hard and took a few gradual steps back, since the car was going at least sixty and showed no signs of slowing down. When Nancy took a few strides backwards as well, farther than I had, I did the same plus another two steps.

Cordelia's face wasn't visible through her windshield at this distance, but her speed said everything about her demeanor. My gaze went to Mr. Lucero as he raised a hand in her direction, and as my heart beat faster as she got closer and closer, I startled at the distinctive sound of the tires rupturing, one *bang* and then a second in quick succession. The car swerved as Cordelia fought for control and to maintain speed despite the vehicle's struggle, the rims scraping the pavement.

The car slowed, but not by enough. Then an arc of electricity crackled across the distance from Mr. Lucero's hand to the hood of the car, slamming into it, causing me to startle again. Smoke drifted from the hood, the engine dying, and his hand remained out in front of him unyieldingly. The car leaned forward, pushing against an invisible force, coming to a gradual stop a few dozen yards in front of my boss.

I realized I'd been holding my breath and let it out in one sharp exhale. "Fucking hell," I whispered.

A low hissing and knocking came from the engine, eventually fading away into nothing, leaving us in a striking silence. I could see Cordelia's face now, and it was the picture of terror, staring at the man in the middle of the road. Mr. Lucero raised both of his hands, making a gradual pushing motion, and I saw her jerk in surprise as the car slid to its left, off the road and through the entrance to the parking lot. Then he lowered his arms to his sides and walked to the car, prompting her to avert her gaze downward, and he stopped beside the hood.

I watched as another car came down the road and looked at the faces of the driver and passenger, who gave us all a curious glance but didn't slow.

Mr. Lucero didn't speak, just looked intently at Cordelia as she stared at her hands, clutching the wheel in a white-knuckled grip. Nancy walked closer and I did the same, stopping a few yards away. The seconds ticked by and then my boss casually leaned forward and rapped his knuckles on the windshield. Cordelia flinched, the strength draining from her as she was visibly overcome with exhausted despair.

After briefly closing her eyes, she slowly unwrapped her fingers from the wheel and opened the door. She stepped out, shutting it behind her, and my breath caught in my throat when I finally was able to see that she literally had blood on her hands.

As my boss took a few steps forward, she stepped backward, bumping into the car. "What did you do?" he asked, his voice low and furious.

"What I've been planning to do for the past five months," she told him. Cordelia's voice was tight and angry, but her stance betrayed her failed attempt at confidence, unable to meet his gaze. "What needed to be done."

"Are you really just human?"

"Since I was born," she snarked back at him.

At the sound of footsteps behind me, I turned to see Ligeia walking toward us, fury in her eyes. She was in her tunic, water-logged from head to toe, and the front was soaked with blood. My eyes slowly widened at the sight.

"No," Cordelia whispered shakily, drawing my gaze back to her. Her face became twisted with rage, a shockingly stark contrast to the reserved, polite woman I'd first met at the bar. "No, no, no, *you were dead!*" she shrieked, lunging forward. Mr. Lucero didn't miss a beat, his hand up and shoving her abdomen back against the car with telekinesis. "You were dead this time, I made sure!" She seemed to not even notice or care about the supernatural restraint, flailing violently in the siren's direction, as if aching to wrap her hands around her throat.

"It's been quite some time since someone tried to kill me," Ligeia said, a note of irritation in her tone. "You made a damn good go of it, for sure." Cordelia slumped back against the car despondently, and tears started streaming down her face. "Who are you?" the siren asked.

Cordelia let out a sob that turned into a manic chuckle. "Yeah, it's amazing how different you look when you chop off all your blonde hair and dye what's left black." She shook her head. "The first and last time you saw me, this past winter, I shot you. Does that ring a bell?"

Ligeia's eyes widened, and she gave the woman standing before her a once-over.

"You said she was dead *this time*," Mr. Lucero stated. "Why did you try to kill her before?"

"Because she killed my sister."

A heavy blanket of oppressive silence descended over us, and I looked to Ligeia in shock. But she only looked annoyed. "I didn't kill anyone."

"Do you really believe that?" Cordelia growled. "You think what you did was a loophole?"

"If I may be so bold as to ask for the story of this supposed murder?" Mr. Lucero said, taking a step closer to Cordelia and glaring at her.

Her face twitched but she seemed to be growing less scared and more resigned. "What does it matter?" she asked. "I failed. I'm sure I'll be seeing my sister in a few minutes, as long as all this doesn't get me sent to Hell."

"Summary execution is not part of my job," he told her. "You'll be taken into custody."

"Right, like you're gonna call the cops about this. I'm not that gullible."

"I didn't say the local police would be the ones arresting you," he said.

Cordelia's eyes flicked up to meet his briefly and I watched as dread gradually weighed down her shoulders.

"She just tried to kill me," Ligeia snapped. "If I'd had my way, I would've broken her neck *before* I was stabbed and drowned. I demand retribution."

Mr. Lucero looked at her sternly. "That is not how this place works. And it is certainly not happening until I learn more about this vendetta. Would you care to enlighten me?"

Ligeia just pursed her lips in annoyance, but Cordelia spoke up. "Her name was Maya," she said, her voice cracking. I looked to the siren and then back to Cordelia, who was staring at the ground, clearly recalling a memory. "We were hiking…we went every time she visited…and we started to hear really beautiful music up ahead. We kept going, and up the path, near a ridge, we saw a woman was the one playing a flute." Cordelia's eyes flicked to Ligeia. "Her."

"It was me, was it?" the siren asked, cocking her head.

"I stopped, but Maya kept walking," the woman continued, ignoring the interruption. "She walked up to her and reached out, with the most…captivated look on her face. Like Ligeia was the most beautiful thing in the world. I didn't get it; for some reason it wasn't affecting me. Like it was only targeting her. I don't know what Ligeia was saying," she said, her voice becoming more despairing with each sentence. "I kept calling Maya's name and she was acting like she couldn't hear me. I went up to her and grabbed her arm, but it was like she didn't recognize me."

Cordelia took in and let out a shaky breath, looking back down at her feet. "Then Ligeia said, 'You're atrocious. This planet would be better off if every human dropped dead.' And she turned and walked away." She sniffed, her lower lip trembling as she started to tear up. "But Maya looked devastated, just inconsolable. I had no idea what was going on. She was frantic, trying to apologize to Ligeia, and I don't even know what for, telling Ligeia she loved her and please not to go, and…and all Ligeia said back was how worthless my sister was, that nobody could ever love someone like her."

She took a breath. "She shoved my sister to the ground and then just…casually walked off. I helped Maya to her feet and started shouting after Ligeia. I was furious, swearing after her, but I don't even remember what I said. Because I turned back around in time to see my sister walk up to the edge of the ridge…and jump."

Staring at Cordelia in stunned silence, I blinked back tears and looked to Ligeia. "What did you do?" I whispered.

"Whoever this insane woman thinks I am, she's wrong," the siren spoke, staring at Cordelia through narrowed eyes.

"I bent over the edge of the ridge and was screaming for her," Cordelia continued through her tears, "but Maya had landed in a bloody heap, and she wasn't moving. There was…*so* much blood. So, I ran after Ligeia. I didn't even realize I'd taken my gun from my bag until it was in my hand. I caught up to her as she reached the parking lot and I was screaming, demanding to know what the *fuck* she'd done. Telling her that she'd killed my sister. But she just said, 'I didn't push her. She jumped.'

"Then I shot her in the back," she continued numbly. "Four times. She collapsed, but then she screamed. Not just in pain. In anger. Then she stood up." Cordelia snapped her eyes back to the woman. "She looked at me like I was a minor irritation, and then stood there for maybe five seconds, looking at where the bullets had exited through the front of her tunic. It was like I wasn't there, like I was just an annoyance, a mosquito that had bitten her. She muttered something to herself…and then just…turned and kept walking. Got into her car and drove off."

"That's a heart wrenching story," Ligeia sighed. "How did you even find out about this gathering? None of us would speak of it to anyone, especially not a human."

Cordelia choked out a laugh. "This place? You really are that stupid. I've been stalking you for two months. There's a tracker on your car. I got the license plate off your car that day, you moronic bitch."

Ligeia stilled, staring at Cordelia, and didn't speak.

"Everywhere you went, I followed," she continued. "I thought you'd caught on when you left your car at a beach for nine days. But then you just walked out of the ocean at sunrise one morning, casual as can be, naked as a jaybird. You pulled on your tunic, got in your car, and left. That was the biggest hint at what you were, spending so much time out there. And I watched you play your flute on the beach at night. I watched as two other people, a woman and a man, walked up to you and then, looking as inconsolable as my sister the last time I saw her face, they walked into the water and never came back out."

"You're saying she murdered two more humans?" Mr. Lucero asked sharply.

"I haven't murdered anyone," Ligeia snarled at him.

"Oh, the wall of information I've got in my living room says otherwise," Cordelia told her, an icy joy coloring her tone. "And I've got photos of them. I've got photos of you every day that I saw you, going back two months. Apparently when you're incredibly powerful and can make humans do whatever you want, you start to think you're untouchable. Made my job easy, at least. Maybe there's hope for humans fighting back against things like you after all, if even someone like me could get this far."

Ligeia's fists were clenched at her sides, and she simmered in a silent rage. I swallowed hard as I saw Mr. Lucero's expression, carved from granite, glowering fiercely at the siren. "Ligeia," he finally spoke, his voice low and tight. "I'm taking you into my custody."

The siren looked at him, her eyes widening. "You wouldn't dare," she whispered. "Just because some insane human spun you a tale?" He didn't reply. "She's the one who broke hospitality. She believed she'd been successful, that she murdered me on hotel grounds. The fact that she was too incompetent to finish the job has no relevance." Mr. Lucero still didn't speak, and it looked like that was starting to bother Ligeia. "Either you take her into custody, or I'm declaring that you've violated your duties as custodian of the crossroads!"

Silence.

In the blink of an eye, Ligeia shoved her hands in Mr. Lucero's direction, but it was clear he'd been anticipating the attack, because even quicker than she'd been, his right hand twisted in her direction.

Her head spun on her neck 180 degrees with a sickening *crack*, and she collapsed to the ground.

As that happened, Mr. Lucero stumbled, his hand coming down on the hood of the car to stabilize himself, and then he vomited.

"Oh my god," I shouted, bolting over to him. "Are you okay?"

He swallowed hard and nodded, taking a deep breath and spitting a few times before wiping his mouth with the back of his hand. "Yes, thank you. I'm all right. She just…managed to grab me for a moment in her attack. I'm fine."

"Grab you?"

Mr. Lucero took another slow breath. "She can control water," he said wearily. "Having someone grab at the water molecules in your body is unpleasant."

My face contorted in horror as that sunk in, and Nancy came over to my side, briefly squeezing my shoulder. Then I glanced at Cordelia, who was staring, pale-faced, at Ligeia's body.

"Is she dead?" she rasped.

"No, it's not that easy," my boss answered, taking one last long, steadying breath and standing up straight.

Reaching into a pocket in his suit's jacket, he took out a pair of handcuffs. Rather than the kind I typically saw on television shows, these were thicker, bronze, and there was something written on them, carved into the metal. Mr. Lucero walked over and knelt next to her, turning her onto her stomach and pulling her wrists together and cuffing them. My gorge rose at the sight of her head facing the wrong way and I quickly averted my eyes.

"Marjorie," he said, walking back over to me. I looked up, meeting his gaze. "I believe everything is resolved. The crossroads is no longer locked down; I can feel it. Rather than make a spectacle of things, I'm going to take a side door to bring Ligeia to where she needs to go."

After seeing the display of his abilities with doors, I knew what that meant, and I nodded. "Understood."

"Please escort Cordelia to my office. I'll meet you there shortly," he said. Turning back to the car, he raised his hands, moving it again telekinetically just far enough into the parking lot to navigate it into the nearest open spot. I stared, knowing that seeing him do anything like that would always be incredible, even if I worked here for forty years.

At the eruption of a grotesque, fleshy cracking sound, I startled, and Cordelia gasped and stumbled a few steps back. I looked over to Ligeia and saw that her neck was fully healed. But she didn't move. She just stared, her fists clenched in the cuffs that tightly restrained her.

"Nancy, once we're gone, you can return to your post," Mr. Lucero told her.

"Will do," she said with a small nod.

At that, Mr. Lucero took hold of Ligeia's left arm and hoisted her to her feet. Her expression was frosty indifference, and she ignored all of us as he escorted her to the right, heading for one of the emergency exit doors.

"Manager," Nancy said softly, drawing my attention. She motioned with her head toward Cordelia. "Go ahead. I'll speak with you later."

Sighing, I walked over to Cordelia, who looked unsteady, her face puffy and red from anger and tears. I hesitated at the blood on her hands, but it wasn't as if germs were an issue for me anymore, so I held my hand out to her. "Let's go."

"Will I… Is he going to kill me?"

My face relaxed into a smile. "No," I said. "That's not how we do things. But there's pretty obviously a conversation to be had." I motioned with my fingers in an invitation, and she took a deep breath, appearing to build up her nerve enough to reach out and take my hand. I led her back toward the hotel's entrance.

Chapter 13

Cordelia and I received some glances as we went inside, but nothing intense. My mind took a moment to try and explain why the diner customers and our guests hadn't all been pressed up against the windows, staring at the spectacle outside, but then I filed it away for later. I briefly met Josh's gaze, nodding at him once, my expression serious but letting him know things were under control. From the concern on his face, he'd definitely seen Ligeia storm through the lobby and walk outside with blood soaked down the front of her tunic, and now he saw the blood on Cordelia's hands. But he just nodded back.

Once Cordelia and I reached the end of the hall, I released her hand and absently wiped the blood on my black pants. Then I opened the door to the stairwell, and she hesitated, but followed me in. I took the keys that I keep on my belt on a small carabiner, passing the stairs and going over to a large metal door.

"Mr. Lucero lives here," I told her, sparing her a glance. "It's a two-story apartment. I don't often need to go to his office, but I do have access for emergencies."

Selecting a key, I unlocked the door, revealing a bare-bones foyer that matched the hotel décor on the other side. Cordelia continued following my lead. There was one door that opened to the walkway outside, which served as a business entrance, and the other door was one that clearly led to a home. Taking another key, I unlocked and then opened it, walking in.

The office was windowless but well-lit, with flush mount lights as well as two hanging light fixtures. There was a handcrafted brown maple desk, well-crafted but not outlandishly large, with one table lamp and a desktop computer. The room had a classic dark wood floor, coffered ceiling and wall paneling, and a pale, geometric-patterned rug that complemented the room's design.

On either side of my boss's desk were bookshelves, tastefully organized with dozens of books as well as various items, some of which were decorative bookends but some likely held meaning that went over my head. There were also over a dozen file cabinets built into the far wall. I guessed that after a few centuries you accumulate a lot of paperwork, and I assumed much of it was elsewhere. Perhaps in a warehouse or two.

Two loveseats sat at a slight angle in front of the desk, with a spare in the corner for crowded occasions. I closed the door and took a seat in one of the chairs, crossing my ankles and loosely clasping my hands in my lap. I sat silently for a long moment before quietly saying, "I'm sorry about your sister."

Cordelia folded her arms tightly. "Thanks," she muttered. Her gaze drifted along the bookshelves, though there wasn't anything more interesting than you'd find in any human's office. I'd done the same thing when I'd first been in here.

"You were really good," I said with a hint of a smirk. "Delayed flight. Cheating husband."

"I actually had a cheating husband, but it was in my early twenties. Advice online says if you're pretending to be someone else, it's best to keep to the truth as much as possible." She shrugged. "I'm just living the single life right now. When I called and found out the sirens had booked the whole hotel, I'd planned on sleeping in my car. I didn't... I mean, I wasn't sure what I'd be walking into. But all I needed to do that first night to get my game face on was think about the day Maya died. Then tears were easy."

She met my gaze for a moment before averting her eyes, looking down at her hands. "I actually had fun that night, though. Eating good food...getting tipsy, but not too drunk...losing at Scrabble... They were nice, and as far as they thought, I was just a new friend. I didn't even see Ligeia until the next morning."

"You knew what she could do and you still decided to stalk her, go after her while she was among her own kind, and kill her?" I asked.

Pausing for a long moment, Cordelia looked over to meet my gaze. She looked tired. "Whatever it took. I didn't know everything, though. I didn't know about that water molecule...skill. Plus, I doubt that controlling the water in people would've even occurred to me." Letting out a long breath, she walked over and sat in the other chair. "You *are* human, right?"

"Yup," I said with a nod. I left out the 'dead' part, figuring that would be piling on at this point. "All the employees are, for logistical reasons. I grew up in Dallas."

"How'd you get into this? How do humans end up knowing about this stuff, working at this hotel?"

"It's different for everyone. I was moving, on my way to start a job I would've hated, and my car broke down nearby," I lied, falling back on the story I'd believed for two years. "Got to talking with the woman who was the Manager then, saw some of the weird stuff around the hotel while I waited to get my car fixed. And she told me she was retiring soon. Long story short, this place was a perfect fit for me. That was two years ago. Some of the other employees…have had a worse introduction. Not my place to say."

Cordelia nodded her understanding and fell silent for a few beats, leaving us with the faint hum of the air conditioner. "It's not fair," she finally muttered. "That we didn't know. That they exist and that one of them could kill Maya, could kill the others, and just…walk away. How many people get killed because we don't know?"

"Not many." She looked at me skeptically and I nodded that it was true. "Your sister had really bad luck," I said, grimacing in angry sympathy. "If nonhumans caused this sort of trouble regularly, how long do you think it would be before knowledge of their existence was commonplace?" I shook my head. "If they're on Earth, the rules are that humans are not fair game. If they break the rules, they die. No prison. No second chances."

"Wait…really?" she asked. "Ligeia, she'll be executed?"

"Yeah. I only learned that recently, because it's so uncommon that I didn't *have to* know," I explained. "When you work here, you respect the guests' privacy. Even as the Manager, I'm on a need-to-know basis. But meeting and interacting with them every day for two years, they're seldom even rude. It's logical, in the end. Whether they're here for business or pleasure, this is a pretty cool planet. I'd want to visit too."

Cordelia considered that for a moment before relenting, giving me a small smile.

We both turned toward the door that led to the apartment as footsteps echoed across the wood floorboards on the other side. Then the door opened, and Mr. Lucero walked in. "Glad to see you've made yourselves comfortable," he said, shutting the door behind him before walking over to his desk and taking a seat in his rolling chair. "First of all…is Cordelia really your name?"

My face went slack, and I looked over to the woman in surprise, but she nodded. "Yeah. Everything else I checked in under was fake. I changed my last name, but I kept the same first name on the ID. I'm sure I would've slipped up if I'd tried to be that complicated."

That made sense. Whoever she was, she wasn't a professional secret agent. The more she made up, the more she would've had to remember. And messing up just once meant she could've been killed.

Mr. Lucero nodded once. "All right. Thank you for coming clean about that. Ligeia is in custody, under lock and key, as you'd say. If you were curious, it was not a targeted attack," he said softly. "Ligeia didn't know you. She seems to harbor a deep hatred for humans, and what they've done to the oceans the past hundred years. As old and powerful as she is, she didn't think much of the murders she was committing. Until they were being revealed in front of someone like me, of course, who could ensure she faced consequences."

Cordelia didn't seem to know what to make of that.

"I'll return to where I left her after we're done here, to explain the bulk of the situation," he told us. "This just takes priority."

"What exactly is it that takes priority?" Cordelia asked. I noticed her arms were folded again and she was tense.

"You won't face any repercussions for your actions," he told her. "Ligeia will be tried and executed for her crimes." She blinked and her eyes widened at the matter-of-fact declaration. "I'd like to have Nancy, the woman who runs the sundry shop, accompany you back to your home to collect the evidence you accumulated. If you bring it to me, you can explain everything you have, and I can record a video of your testimony as an eyewitness. I'm afraid you can't be present at the trial, though, since you're human."

Cordelia stared at him. "You're…really not going to…arrest me or anything? For what I did?"

Mr. Lucero shook his head. "Do you know what this place is?" he asked.

She glanced at me and then back to him. "You mean the hotel?"

"Exactly. You didn't even know this is venerated ground," he said. "You will have the rules of hospitality explained to you, but there will be no actual punishment. Unfortunately, you will be banned from the crossroads after the trial. It means if you try to return, you'll simply pass through the intersection as if nothing is here. That's not up to me. But if you'd attempted to kill Ligeia elsewhere in retribution for murdering your sister and two other humans, there would've been no repercussions whatsoever."

"So, I'm banned from the hotel because I…violated the rules that keep everyone here safe?" Cordelia asked slowly, relaxing a bit and leaning back in her chair.

"Yes, but you'll not just be banned from the hotel. I said you will be banned from the *crossroads*, which is its own entity," he explained, motioning vaguely in the direction of the other buildings and shops.

"Wait, this-this whole place is a nonhuman place?" she asked.

"It is," he replied. "The crossroads will allow me the time to go through the evidence you have and go through with the trial, since your presence is necessary. But you will be banned afterward. The entity will not allow someone who violated the rules so severely to come and go as they please. And for the record, I am human. I'm just also…more."

Cordelia paused for a moment. "You said she would be executed," she said. "But you also said there would be a trial."

"There will be a trial, but I already know what the outcome will be," he replied. "The fact that she attempted to kill me, that is another crime in and of itself, and one that is more severe considering my position as the custodian of the crossroads. That makes her fate inevitable. We'll still have the trial for the same reason humans have them even when the outcome is a foregone conclusion. We don't simply march an accused person to their death. Evidence needs to be presented, and those in power need to be informed in a…an official way that follows procedure."

"Sometimes a guilty person has a lawyer that gets them off on a technicality."

Slowly and deliberately, Mr. Lucero told her, "Our justice system is different from America's in several ways." He paused before continuing, "I'm assuming you have a contingency in place to send the evidence to someone you trust, in case you were killed at the hotel?"

Cordelia's face went slack, and she hesitated. "Maybe," she hedged.

"You can keep it in place until you're satisfied justice has been done," he said. "I just wanted to ensure it isn't triggered unnecessarily." She paused but then nodded her agreement. "Nancy's shift ends at five o'clock. You can drive the two of you back to your home for the evidence. Until then, you can go speak to any friends you've made while you were here. Explain the situation."

Shifting in her chair, she winced. "You think they'll be angry? About what I tried to do? And that I lied about everything?"

"Not as angry as you think they will be," he answered. "After learning what Ligeia did, it's likely they'll be grateful to have learned of her true colors, when in fact one of them might have started a relationship and left with her on Saturday."

That seemed to give Cordelia a new perspective, and she thought on that for a moment. "That makes sense. Look, I understand why I can't be at the trial, that it's somewhere humans aren't allowed," Cordelia said, "but I won't believe she's dead unless I see her die with my own eyes."

Mr. Lucero nodded slowly. "I expected nothing less. You'll be permitted to be present for the execution. On that topic, I was curious about your train of thought. Why did you attempt to kill her the way you did?"

Cordelia flinched and looked down, obviously uncomfortable with an open discussion about it. She gathered her thoughts for a long moment. "There really are no stories about how to kill sirens," she admitted. "I did a ton of research, must have read and studied every story written about them three times. The only thing I learned that involved them dying is when sailors escaped the sound of their singing, they threw themselves into the sea in despair. So…I figured drowning was my best bet. I…"

She closed her mouth, letting out a breath through her nose, before speaking again, still staring at her hands. "I've been flirting with her, pretending I was interested. I asked to go to her room for a drink. I was…behind her, so I took out my knife and I slit her throat, and while she was struggling with that, I stabbed her in the heart," she whispered. "Then I did it again. When she actually collapsed, quickly losing a lot of blood…I dragged her into the bathroom and into the tub. It was already full, so I pushed her underwater until…until she stopped moving."

The room was weighted with silence when she stopped talking. Mr. Lucero nodded. "That's quite clever." Cordelia just pursed her lips. "How do you feel, knowing sirens live on Earth and can do whatever they wish to humans?"

Her gaze darted up to him. "What? I… You mean the others here? Or are there… Marjorie said they aren't allowed to hurt humans. It's ironclad law."

He nodded again, just once. "Indeed. And it's rare. But that wasn't my question."

Cordelia stared at him curiously. "It's…scary," she finally said. "But it sounds like they take the laws more seriously than humans take ours. When it comes to hurting humans, at least; Marjorie didn't mention how they treat each other back…wherever they live. And, I mean, humans can do whatever they want to each other too. So, I figure I'm a lot more likely to get murdered by a human." She shrugged. "Which is comforting to know, after what I saw happen to my sister."

"A reasonable position to take." He leaned forward, forearms on his desk and hands clasped, looking contemplative. "I ask because I wanted to know if this was about justice, or if you had built up a hatred for nonhumans in general. Because, as you now know, there are some humans at the crossroads who know about the nonhumans who live on or visit Earth. But there are also others elsewhere who know," he told her. "Very few, of course, but they're all over the world. They are our eyes and ears, invisible, because whatever they are, all humans seem identically harmless to those who are more powerful. And I wanted to present you with the opportunity to become one of them."

I blinked, stunned, and then looked at Cordelia, who seemed even more astonished. Just a few minutes earlier, she'd been worried of repercussions, and now she was being told even more confidential information. Now she was being invited into the fold. "You're asking me to be…what, a spy?" she asked.

"More like a private investigator," Mr. Lucero replied. "Part-time. There is risk involved, but it's minor. Most of what you would do is exactly the kind of work you did following Ligeia, up to and *not* including your trip to the hotel. You did all of that with no training, correct? What do you do for work?"

Cordelia shrugged and gave a small smile. "Information architect." He raised an eyebrow. "Yeah, not exactly something you say you want to be when you're eight. It's just computer stuff. I basically organize information on websites, software, that kind of work. It sounds boring to most people, but I love it. I got my bachelor's in computer science."

"Then what you accomplished is extremely impressive, even though your survival was also due to a large amount of luck," he told her. "I'd be interested to see what you're capable of if you *had* training." Cordelia's expression turned introspective, and she leaned back in her chair.

"She just avenged her sister's death and could've been killed," I said tightly. "Shouldn't she be allowed to go back to her life? To just…do what she wants?"

Mr. Lucero nodded. "She can. This is just an offer."

"How many of these PIs have been killed doing this job?" I demanded.

"Marjorie, it's okay," Cordelia said, her tone somewhere between surprised and reassuring. "It's not like I'm going to make the decision right now. And the way he explained it, I'm not shocked he asked. It makes sense."

I shrugged dismissively. "It's just…were you happy? Doing that computer work, hanging with your friends, dating, whatever. Could you still have what you want in life if you do this?"

I couldn't help myself, feeling compelled to ask these questions. People who were hurt by this world, mentally or physically, sometimes couldn't go back to the way things were. Prime examples were Fyfe and Andrea, and of course, me. Even though mine was a particularly severe kind of one-way street. But Cordelia? She had just gotten closure. She could move on.

"Did you explain how you came to work here, Marjorie?" Mr. Lucero asked me quietly, drawing my gaze.

Tensing, I swallowed hard, seeing Cordelia look back and forth from him to me. "Your car breaking down?" she asked, her eyes narrowing.

My boss's expression didn't so much as twitch as she revealed my lie. It seemed my feelings on this topic and why I had them were obvious to him. That shouldn't have surprised me. He wasn't an idiot. But he was still letting me take the lead, allowing me to decide whether or not I explained my concerns to her.

I chose not to.

"It's just…a little more complicated than I said," I muttered. Taking in and letting out a deep breath, I met her worried gaze. "I love it here. But I can't go back to the life I had hoped for when I drove away from my parents' house two years ago. I just wanted to make sure you take your time and consider this decision. Okay?"

Cordelia nodded slowly, examining my expression. "Okay." She smiled. "Thanks for looking out for me."

In that moment, I became starkly aware of our age difference, that she was at least ten years older than me. It was likely she'd already made a bunch of decisions that changed her life, ones that she couldn't go back and fix, and that she had regrets. She'd already mentioned being married and divorced because of an affair. Some of the tension drained out of my shoulders as a little sheepishness burrowed its way in, and I mentally jotted this down as one more thing to mention when I started therapy.

"As Marjorie said, take time to think about it," Mr. Lucero said. "And not just over the next few days. Once you go home, you can settle back into your old life, and it will probably be a few weeks before I'll be in touch to ask for your decision. For now, you'll continue to stay in your room here. Marjorie will walk you back, and you can speak to the guests about what happened when you feel ready." Cordelia gave him a tight nod in reply.

My boss turned to me, smiling. "As for you, Manager, thank you for your support with this incident. Now…I believe you have a hotel to run. Fyfe, in particular, needs to be informed."

I winced and closed my eyes, shaking my head. That was true; it was time to break out the hazmat suit again and deal with Ligeia's room. Fyfe would definitely need to rip up and replace the areas of carpeting where an artery's worth of blood had soaked through. I opened my eyes, sighing, and smiled back at my boss knowingly. "Yes, sir."

Epilogue

When I told Fyfe he needed to report to a blood-drenched room for cleanup, he took it in stride, less distressed about the fact that it was necessary and more that it had been from an attempted murder. I met him and Andrea in the break room after her shift that night, explaining the basics of what had happened.

As you might have guessed, Andrea seemed the most quietly furious of the two, and when I mentioned Cordelia would be present to ensure Ligeia was indeed executed, she simply said, "Good."

Also, I went to Nancy the next day when I started my shift. She looked up to me with a hint of a smirk that said she knew what I was going to ask. "Something I can help you with, Manager?"

I pursed my lips in a smile right back at her. "Mr. Lucero… He said wizards don't need wands."

"No, they don't," she replied, closing the magazine in her hand. "Witches do, though."

"Right. What's the difference?"

"Witches are potential, sometimes left untapped. Wizards are power."

Mulling that over for a moment, I nodded, pretty sure I understood the gist of what that meant. "When you were with us, I couldn't tell at first what you did. But it was why no one noticed what was going on, wasn't it?"

Nancy nodded. "It's a spell, to make humans see something different, something normal. You've seen shapeshifters, who can change to look human. And you've seen glamours, though you haven't noticed. That's an innate magic someone has, that twists reality. A spell is the third way to camouflage someone or something."

"Glamour," I echoed quietly. Josh had mentioned those. The descriptions she'd given me were fascinating, all the more so because I still hardly knew anything about them. "Thank you," I told her. "For all of that and for…for being there."

The older woman gave me a genuine smile. "Of course."

When it was time for our guests to leave, they left gradually over the course of the day, with some wanting to get an early start and others preferring to sleep in and take their time. And perhaps have one last seafood meal at the diner. I saw many of them leaving in pairs and I smiled at the thought of the little baby sirens that would be born out there, somewhere oceanside and remote.

When Parthenope checked out, she was with another siren whose name I had forgotten, since I hadn't seen her much. As I took back their key cards, I spoke up to her. "Thank you. For everything. It was enough just having backup with that local, but what you said to me on the roof," I said quietly, "it really helped me."

To my surprise, Parthenope looked confused. "Sorry?"

I hesitated. "The local that you made pass out? And then later, when I talked to you on the roof?"

She slowly shook her head. "I've, um, been a bit of a hermit. I met Himerope at the swimming hole after a few days, and we've mostly kept to ourselves. Was it…a dream you're thinking of, perhaps?"

Flummoxed, I blinked a few times before looking to Josh, who looked just as baffled. "Uh…no. No, for sure it wasn't a dream."

"Hm." She thought for a moment before saying, "Perhaps someone who wanted to help, then. It sounds like they did."

"Uh, y-yeah," I managed. "She- They- They helped, for sure."

At that, she smiled happily and then left with Himerope, holding hands.

"So…that happened," Josh said slowly.

I didn't reply. But that night, I went back up to the roof. Iktomi's cocoon was gone, and I smiled, glad she'd healed up and gone on her way.

The curl of an arm of our galaxy spread across the darkness above, like a painting from the universe itself. Walking to the middle of the roof, I stared up at the stars and distant galaxies. Wondering if somewhere in the vast universe, there was another planet with life like ours. And whether they had their own mysterious visitors.

"I figured it was risky," came a quiet, amused voice behind me.

I didn't startle, because I was hoping to see her, but I promptly turned around in surprise that she'd actually come. A woman stood near the edge of the roof, leaning against the short brick wall, a soft smile on her face. Her long, wavy black hair was the darkest I'd ever seen, reaching her waist, and she wore a ruched satin dress the color of gold, with purple fringe.

"You're…her," I said, more curious than anything. "Both times, it wasn't Parthenope."

"Yes. I felt you calling to me just now and thought I'd formally meet you. It's nice to finally meet you, Marjorie," she said. "I hope it wasn't disconcerting, realizing you hadn't been talking to your guest."

Honestly, it had been in the moment, but after a few minutes, it had settled in with all the other oddness in my life. Now I was more curious about the gorgeous woman on the roof with me, who appeared dressed for a dinner party where they drank glasses of wine worth more than my savings account. "No, it was…fine. Nice to meet you too," I said. "Who are you, exactly?"

"You can call me Cate." She walked over to stand beside me, tilting her head up to look at the stars just as I had. "I've been attentive to the changes here these past few years. We've spoken before several times, but only in passing. You and this place are very much…in my wheelhouse, as you'd say."

"Oh," I murmured in comprehension. "Well, thank you, Cate. I've been going through a difficult time. What you did, and what you said, it was really kind of you."

Her smile widened and she looked over to me. "I simply spoke the truth. Some of us whom you meet, our lives are…designed. Destined. We can make choices, like my decision to speak to you, and to tell you the truth now, but who we are changes little and slowly over our lives. Especially the entities like the crossroads, which are something else entirely. It's ageless, almost completely fixed. I've always felt a combination of envy and pity for humans, who have so many tiny choices that alter the trajectory of their lives. Billions of you, each your own utterly different story. And having an astonishing array of options in your life, but often, still having very little control."

I nodded slowly. "It can be quite the roller coaster."

"Indeed." Cate's gaze moved to look over the buildings at the crossroads. "I'm fond of your crossroads. Over the centuries, it's taught me much about those who live here, and those who visit, and the interactions between them. Now I have someone new. Someone unique," she spoke, looking over to me. "It's been delightful watching you make this your home, seeing you embrace your second life and become part of the crossroads. I'm confident that you'll continue to do well."

"Thanks," I murmured, warmth curling in my chest at her confidence. My future still seemed so scary, even having so much of it planned out, much as a nonhuman would. Looking back to the sky, I let out a long breath. Astronomy has never been my strong suit. It was moments like this that I wished I knew more. "Can you visit them?" I asked faintly. "All the planets around all those stars? It must be magical."

Turning back when she didn't reply, looking around the roof, I realized Cate had vanished. I sighed. "Enjoy wherever you're off to next. Hope to see you soon."

Stepping up onto the picnic table bench, I lay down on the table, folding my hands on my belly. And I stared at the stars until I reached that dizzying point where I felt both unimaginably big and incredibly small.

Milton Keynes UK
Ingram Content Group UK Ltd.
UKHW021803270524
443037UK00001B/23